JUNE JENSON
AND THE
SHIELD OF QUELL

(BOOK ONE)

EMILY HARPER

ISBN-13 9780992095338

Praise for the June Jenson Series

"Emily Harper has a very distinctive writing style and all of her books have something in common – they contain a lot of laugh-out-loud moments, feisty, opinionated and loveable heroines and a fast-paced action filled storyline."
–Cosmochicklitan

"This is a hugely action-packed book and it's all kinds of ridiculous, in the best sense... my favourite of her novels so far." *–Reviewed the Book*

"Emily Harper has a very distinctive writing style and all of her books have something in common – they contain a lot of laugh-out-loud moments, feisty, opinionated and loveable heroines and a fast-paced action filled storyline."
–Cosmochicklitan

"This is a hugely action-packed book and it's all kinds of ridiculous, in the best sense... my favourite of her novels so far." *–Reviewed the Book*

"June Jenson and the Shield of Quell is a fun story that will have you hooked from page one, with some very lovable quirky main characters and lots of intrigue." *–Alba in Bookland*

"Harper has given life to a wonderful array of characters. Each one helps move the story along and keeps us entertained with their antics." *–Whispering Stories*

White Lies

"With humour, romance and a great story that flowed flawlessly this is a debut not to be missed." –*Mrs Mommy Booknerd*

"It's a book I could easily see becoming a fun summer movie, filled with lots of fantastic shoes." –*Readers' Favorite Reviews*

Checking Inn

"A tragicomic novel about lies, deception and colour-coded pens." –*She Loves to Read*

"Emily Harper does a fantastic job of creating this quirky character who you can't help but laugh at and root for all at the same time." –*Readers' Favorite Reviews*

My Sort-of, Kind-of Hero

"It has this feel-good heart-warming touch that will leave you grinning like a toon… Emily is quickly becoming one of my favourite Chick Lit authors, with fresh stories and lovable characters." –*Addictive ChickLit*

"It is a chick lit with a difference." –*The Book Corner*

For Ava and Noah. Whether we are casting spells, having daring sword fights, or hosting fancy tea parties, you will always be my life's greatest adventure. Thanks for letting Mommy be a part of the magic.

ACKNOWLEDGMENTS

This series has been simmering in my mind for years, and it seems surreal that the day is finally here when I can hold this book in my hands and know that I've finally done it.

I want to say a huge thank you to my wonderful writer's group: Linda, Dan and Erika. Thank you for reading this book and pushing me to make it the best novel I could write.

To my wonderful editor, Emily Ferko, you always make the stories that much better.

To my friends and family who constantly have to listen to me go over plot points, cover design, and font sizes. I do appreciate that I sound crazy most of the time, but thanks for never pointing it out.

And finally, to David, Ava and Noah. Our family is a fine balance of love, laughter and crazy– just the way I like it.

Chapter One

"You're in."

I clutch the phone tightly with one hand and grope the ledge of the nearby table for support.

Some sort of garbled noise escapes from my throat, which I really hope gets lost somewhere in electronic space before it meets the person at the other end of the line.

"Be at the Ashmolean on Beaumont Street in an hour," the voice tells me. The line disconnects before I even have a chance to speak.

I slowly replace the phone and push my glasses further up the bridge of my nose.

That probably could have gone slightly smoother. Like I could have actually said *something*. But I console myself with the knowledge that I didn't do anything really embarrassing, like shout for joy, or thank them profusely. Surely saying *nothing* is better.

Surely.

"Who was that?" I hear a gruff voice call from the other room. "If it's that bloody alumni calling again, you tell them I'm not giving them a bloody cent! They've already had the best years of my bloody life, but that's not enough for them, is it?"

"It wasn't for you!" I yell back.

Because everything in life isn't about *you*, I grumble in my head.

"Where's the bloody whiskey?" he yells again, and the sound of a bottle clinking against glass greets my ears. This can only mean one thing: he found the key to the small drinks cabinet. Again.

"You are not to be drinking with your medication!" I yell. "I wrote that in your book last week."

Telling myself to calm down, I lean backwards against the large round hall table. I've always thought it was too traditional for the Professor to have his telephone in the main hallway like this, perched on the table. He would never even consider a portable one. But now I am grateful for its solitary position given I have a moment alone to process this without having him ask me what is going on. Staring at nothing in particular I look at the wall, counting my blessings over my challenges, just like that lovely psychologist who charges me a fortune tells me to do. Another clatter comes from the other room and my eyes slowly rise to the pictures that are hanging on the study wall directly in front of me. The clippings of the newspaper articles– very carefully chosen, of course– framed and put up on display for all to admire: his excavation discoveries; his contributions to the development and understanding of Anglo-Saxon history.

That was always his passion, and his degrees showcase this: his two doctorates meant to impress. Of course, the doctorates were never on the wall when I was growing up; he didn't have anything he needed to prove back then. But things change.

I hear some more grumbling and more glass clinking.

Deciding to tackle one thing at a time, I turn to face the phone again, pushing aside the phonebook. The little book really is unnecessary now that the Professor doesn't use the telephone anymore. Not that he used it that much to begin with. Something about the telephone company being the Antichrist– I never did catch on to his reasoning for that one. I recall the number I need from memory and punch it into the phone. There are many benefits to having an eidetic memory, but recalling phone numbers has always been at the top of the list for me. I think of all the poor souls that have to reach for the telephone book, or, even worse, search online to find the number they are looking for. I did some quick math once and I reckon I save about sixteen hours a year. I'd like to say I do something productive with that time, but I save it up until Christmas holidays and just sleep the whole day.

"HomeAid, Janette speaking."

Hearing the bright voice on the other end, I immediately begin to relax.

"I'm so sorry for such late notice, but would you be able to send someone around tonight to keep an eye on my grandfather?" I ask.

"That shouldn't be a problem, we have quite a few nurses available tonight. Could I have your address please?"

I tell her our address and wait while she types something into her computer.

"Oh," I hear from the other end of the line and notice a change in the tone. "We are full up tonight, I'm afraid."

"Full up?" I shake my head. "You said a minute ago it wouldn't be a problem."

"Yes, well, I was mistaken," she says, defensive now.

"How could you be mistaken?" I shout, and when I receive no response I change from angry to pleading. "Please, is there not *anyone* you could send? I have a very important meeting to go to and I just–"

"I'm taking off my trousers!" I hear from the other room and something is flung into the wall– presumably the trousers– "We're obviously not entertaining anyone without any bloody alcohol in the house!"

Janette clears her voice on the other end of the line. "As I said, we're full up."

I stand up straighter. "I would like to speak to someone else, please. Perhaps a supervisor."

"My supervisor will tell you the exact same thing. We're full up."

"You keep saying that, but a moment ago you told me you had plenty of nurses available."

"None that are willing to look after your grandfather, I'm

afraid." The false apology in her voice is even more annoying than when she flat out refused. "You see, HomeAid is equipped to assist the elderly with everyday tasks, however, if we feel our staff is at jeopardy of physical or emotional turmoil we have the right to refuse services."

"My grandfather has never laid a hand on anyone!" I say in outrage.

"No, but his... *vocabulary*... well, we at HomeAid are just not comfortable with it," Janette says. "We also recommend that it might be time to find alternative arrangements for your grandfather's care."

"Alternative arrangements? What are you trying to say?" I ask, but I knew it was only a matter of time before we had a note in our file. *Do not go over there— he is a crotchety old fusspot who has terrible temper tantrums and refuses to wear his trousers.*

"It means that we are full up," she repeats the phrase slowly.

I clench my jaw. These people are supposed to be professionals. They are supposed to be the ones looking out for us when we can no longer look out for ourselves.

"I'll pay double the rate," I say, forgetting for a moment in my desperation the absolute absurdity of the situation. Honestly, there has got to be more objectionable people to look after than my slightly misguided grandfather.

"I guess it would be unreasonable to expect a bloody cup of tea anytime this afternoon!" The Professor yells from the other room and I close my eyes and take a deep breath.

"I'll pay triple," I say in a quiet voice.

"Sorry."

The next thing I know I hear the click on the other end. She hung up on me! Oh, are they going to be receiving a scathing review on Whitepages!

I put the receiver down and look up when I hear shuffling feet approaching.

"June, be a dear and make me something with bacon for tea," he says. He waddles into the room wearing nothing but underpants with Father Christmas's face printed in a small pattern on the buttocks while he holds one of his old journals in his slender hand. "Also, I see here that I'm supposed to have dinner with Thomas tomorrow at seven, but that is utterly impossible. I've scheduled a lecture on the Saxon Invasion for the same time."

He's lost too much weight. He's always been on the slender side, but he isn't eating properly, always turning away his meals. His metal-rimmed glasses, which magnify his crystal blue eyes, are forever perched on the end of his nose as though he is always preparing to read something. His unruly grey hair that is still thick and full is dishevelled on his head even though I just combed it.

"Grandfather– Professor," I quickly right my slip of the tongue before I continue. "That meeting has already been cancelled."

It's been a difficult day for him. Most days the medication works wonders, almost making him whole again.

But then there are other days, like today, that deflate the hope that is nurtured by the better days. The drinking certainly doesn't help matters, either.

"Good," he shuffles across the floor to stand right beside me. "You might make a decent PA after all."

I look into his eyes and squash down my resentment: my resentment for him, for the situation. He knows who I am. I'm June. But right now he has slotted me into the part of his life he is most confident with; right now I am his assistant, and he is a professor again. I wonder where he thinks his granddaughter is, or if he even registers that she exists.

"Now about that whiskey..." he says.

"Professor, I apologise, but we are out of whiskey right now. I'll have someone run out and get some more," I try to mollify him, which only receives more grumbling.

I look down at my watch and pale. How could so much time have gone by already? It is going to take me a quarter of an hour to get to the Ashmolean and I still have no clue what to do with the Professor.

I make a quick decision and try to convince myself it will all work out fine.

"Professor, we need to go out for a quick meeting somewhere, so if you could just put your trousers back on—" I turn him around and lead him back towards the sitting room where he has left the telly on, the news blaring from the small screen with lines running through it. I really should get him a new one, though the news programs only serve to confuse him further. I thought he might be put off of it if he couldn't actually see the screen, but he's just resolved to use it more as a radio.

"Meeting?" he asks, looking down. "Nothing in the journal..."

We both step aside of the newspaper clippings he's left scattered over the floor. One of his journals lays open beside the mess, the pages wrinkled from the glue where he has just attached a new article. The familiar face staring up from the newspaper's article, the face that is missing from all the clippings framed on the Professor's study walls, stares back at me with a sorrowful expression.

Guiding the Professor back to the chair I pat him on the shoulder, smiling at him in a reassuring way.

"It's last minute. A favour for an old friend," I explain, looking around the room for his discarded trousers.

"An old friend of mine, or of yours?" he asks.

I hesitate for a moment. "Yours. An old colleague who would like your opinion on something."

He thinks for a moment, probably wondering if he should ask for a name, but seems to realize he wouldn't remember the name anyways and so shrugs it off.

"I hope you told them we couldn't stay long," he says, reaching for his grey trousers.

"Of course, shouldn't be too long." I hope to God it's not.

While the Professor busies himself with his trouser legs,

I run up the stairs and into my bedroom, my shirt already half off over my head. I scan my wardrobe quickly and wince. Really nothing is suitable. Having said that, I'm not really sure what suitable *is* for this particular occasion. Am I going out to dinner? Is this another test where I'll have to scale some walls, or go through a maze?

Honestly, nothing would surprise me at this point.

Of course I'd heard of the Alliance. Well, heard stories– references really– from some of the library books at Oxford. No one really hears specifics because... well... no one is actually quite sure if they exist. They would still be an urban myth to me if Charles hadn't been so careless and left the file on his desk. I still question why they chose Charles as their recruiter. Not that Charles isn't a really great man, but...

Well, I say he's great because I have to. That's what you have to say when someone asks you about your best friend's abilities and you really have no confidence in them. It would be very unkind to say Charles is where he is in life because of his money and connections. Unkind, but true. He'd be the first one to tell you as much. I'm still convinced he changed the grade my grandfather gave him in Ancient Artefacts, which enabled him to graduate. Not that it matters, I mean, it was one class years ago.

But I know he did it.

I take a step towards the wardrobe and hear a fluttering noise. I look down and see one of the newspaper clippings from the Professor's notebook has attached itself to the bottom of my slipper. I bend down to peel it off and wince when I see the picture. He really shouldn't be looking at these; it doesn't help anything. If anything, it only makes things worse. "Sutton-Hoo Archaeologist Scandal", the headline reads. He's even highlighted the by-line:

"Renowned Oxford Professor, Dr Albert Arthur Jenson, has been implicated in the mystery of the missing piece found in the latest excavation at Sutton-Hoo. His partner, Dr Daniel Cooke, who was first refuting the claims that anything was taken, has now retracted his statement, insisting that he can only be sure of the fact that he himself is innocent."

I close my eyes and breathe in through my nostrils. Today isn't the day for this, but the papers have to go. I have no idea how he got a hold of so many copies. It seems that for every batch I throw out, twenty more suddenly materialize.

I put the faded, brown article onto my bedside table and stand again in order to take off my slippers before I root around in my wardrobe and find my one and only semi-formal outfit. A dark grey pencil skirt dress with leather sleeves that actually helps my tall, lanky frame to appear as though it has some semblance of curves. My dark brown hair is too short to really do anything with, so I tousle it a bit more, the waves falling just past my chin. Another one of life's true cruelties. I've had the same cropped look my whole life because as my grandfather puts it: there are far more beautiful things to look at in this world than a woman's appearance. This loosely translates as: he was too busy studying dead people and their stuff to give a toss about my hairstyle. So as a child I went with the Professor to the man who always cut his hair and I ended up with this. Thirty-plus years going strong. I tried to change it once, in my sophomore year, but the Professor's mind had already started to slip and his doctor advised against any physical changes. *We have to do what we can, June*, he advised. That was the beginning of my life-long guilt trip.

I look in the mirror at my ensemble and shrug. It's not going to get much better than this.

"It's not the right order of things when someone's assistant makes a man late to his own meeting," I hear the yell from downstairs as I'm trying to put my diamond stud through my earlobe. It was the Professor's Christmas present to me last year; I found them in January behind the loveseat.

"Coming! I just have to arrange our car," I yell and pick up my mobile from my purse as I hear the creaking of the stairs.

"Whom did you say I'm meeting again?" he asks, popping his head through the doorframe, looking confused.

The guilt runs through me at the thought of confusing him more with my lies, but the truth is, he won't even remember any of this tomorrow, and my whole future is riding on this evening.

"An old colleague," I say, being as vague as possible.

He pauses for a moment, blinking at me and I can see him trying to create a coherent thought.

"I bet he'll have scotch," he says, turning to walk back out of the room.

Chapter Two

"She gazed upon his eyes and saw into the depths of his soul," the sultry voice breathes from the car's speakers.

"I'm sorry, I don't think I have made myself clear. This is life or death for me. There's got to be some way to get around this," I say, leaning forward from my seat in the back of the hired car.

"Have no fear June, for Professor Albert Arthur Jenson, they will wait," the Professor says from beside me, lifting up the console in between us that is supposed to be used as an armrest. "Where's the bloody minibar in this thing?"

"He swept her limp body into his rippling arms and carried her up the hill."

"If I miss this, that's it!" I lean even further forward, trying to make the driver understand. "They never do this, it's unheard of!"

I look down at the folder in my hands. I'm not really sure why I brought it; everything that is written inside it is permanently etched in my prefrontal lobe. Every face, every ability… even their hobbies. It's there, waiting for me at a moment's notice. One word from my hippocampus and it is right before my eyes.

Maybe I shouldn't bring the folder inside. I mean, that's kind of the whole point of why they asked me to join in the first place. If I bring it in, they might think my mind is not up to the task.

I place the folder in my bag and close the zipper. I must remember not to open that during the meeting, or they might think it's my study notes.

"It's got to be here somewhere," the Professor says, trying to look beneath the seat.

"I really think it was a mistake to get off the motorway." My leg bounces as I push up the nosepiece of my dark rimmed glasses, a nervous habit I have never been able to break.

"Deacon kicked in the door to his vast mansion, leaving the broken piece of wood swinging on its hinges."

"Can we turn this off?" I yell in frustration at the driver.

"Sorry, can't. My agent says that my theatre choices lack emotional turmoil. This was his idea," the driver says, pointing one of his long fingers to the car's speaker.

"You're an actor?" I ask, taking in his floppy brown hair and high cheekbones. I bet he's going for a young Hugh Grant look.

"Playwright," he answers.

"So you listen to Romance 101 on tape, and you copy it?"

"Just getting inspiration," he taps the side of his forehead.

"What are you doing?" I lean forward as he makes a left-hand turn.

"It's blocked ahead. I'm just going to go up Brewer and back down Pembroke."

The narrow lane of Brewer Street only allows our single car up it. The historical buildings flank both sides of our car with their weathered but well-maintained facades. The blue doors of the buildings on the left pass by in a blur.

We stop suddenly. A van blocks the small lane in front of Christ Church Cathedral School, and three men get out to unload something from the back.

I really must stay in the car and calm down.

I must not get out and scream at them to move their bloody vehicle before I take the Professor's umbrella to their front window.

And yet my hand reaches for the handle anyways.

"I don't know this place," the Professor says, looking out the window at the schoolhouse to our left. "I thought you said I was meeting someone."

He scans the street, more searching his mind, I presume, than the seemingly endless walls of stone.

"We're not there yet," I say, and decide that this might be the right time to start broaching the subject that will not be received very favourably. "There has been a bit of a change to the plan, though. I will be going in first for the meeting. Alone."

"Alone?" he asks, puzzled, and then he shrugs it off with

a laugh. "Whatever for? I don't need some longwinded introduction."

"Well, I just have to check on a few things and speak to someone. You can stay in the car and keep— er…"

"Griffin," the driver supplies. "Like the mythological beast."

I blink at him in the rear-view mirror twice before returning to face the Professor. "You can keep *Griffin* company."

"You tricked me!" he says, and immediately starts to reach for the button on his trousers. "You made me put these bloody things on for nothing!"

"I will only be a few minutes," I try to mollify him. "Griffin could take you for a nice little drive if you'd like?"

When I called for the car service I briefly explained the situation and was assured that as long as the meter was still running and the fare climbing, everything would be taken care of.

"Don't bloody patronize me!" He unbuckles his belt. "You don't have to mind me. I'm not a child!"

His eyes catch on his notebook. He seems to know what the book means, even when he can't seem to put anything else into place.

The silence is deafening in the car as the Professor visibly calms down. Forgetting his trousers, he sits up straight in his seat.

"We will go and get whiskey and pick you up on the way

back."

I make no mention of the fact that he isn't supposed to drink with his medication. It makes me worry that he somehow managed to get his hands on some alcohol earlier, which would explain the bad day he is having.

"There might not even be a meeting," I say, looking at the van that refuses to move. "My one chance, my *one* chance and I won't even get the opportunity to blow it."

"Call and say you'll be late," Griffin suggests with a shrug, which causes his floppy brown hair to fall carelessly across his forehead. He probably thinks that haircut gives him an artistic look. Or he's so artistic that he doesn't get his hair cut often, thus giving him an artistic look. I'll have to think that through later, it could be a good logical formula example for my students.

"You think they gave me their *number*?" I laugh at the innocence. "They don't give people their numbers. They're like drug lords, you communicate through people to get to them. They don't tell you their *names,* they certainly don't give you their *numbers.*"

Not that this is illegal. If anything the Alliance is the complete *opposite* to illegal… so… legal. We will be protecting our country's most important artefacts. *Priceless* artefacts.

I lean forward to look at the digital clock and shake my head in disbelief. How can thirty minutes have gone by so quickly? I thought I had managed to leave the house with plenty of time.

"I can't believe this is happening to me," I shake my head in my hands. "We're not even close!"

"Someone should shoot the bloke who approved road work to be done on a Friday night," Griffin replies. "And these tossers; don't they know there is a driveway right up there?"

"Ughh..." I look at the two cars behind me as we all sit at a standstill. "Do you know how hard I have worked to get this chance? I've had to do tests..."

"You mentioned it," he says dryly, and turns up the volume on his romance audiobook.

Well, I feel the tone he just used is a little unfair. I mentioned it *once*. And I was very brief. I mean, obviously you are not supposed to talk about the Alliance.

It's actually the very first rule of the whole organization.

Earlier in the evening, when I first got in the car, I yelled, "As fast as you can!" like they do in the movies. I could tell that Griffin was not going to take my situation seriously. I would have thrown money at him for emphasis, but the hire is on account and everyone knows you don't give the driver a tip *before* you've made the journey. I mentioned that the meeting was very important and when his response was minimal (at best) I subtly implied that I am about to be accepted into a secret alliance.

Subtly implied meaning I told him I was being accepted into a secret alliance.

Obviously I didn't mention them by name, though.

He still didn't seem to take anything to heart so I told him that I went through vigorous testing for six months in order to be asked to join.

He didn't seem impressed with that either, which might explain why he's not the best playwright. I mean this could be a story for the ages! It's certainly the story of my life.

Joining the Alliance, well, it's my lifelong dream. I mean, yes, technically I have only known it has existed for the past six months, and yes I had to beg Charles to even bring up my name in the recruiting process. But still, if I had known about it my whole life I would have wanted to do it for that long.

From what very little I was able to glean about the Alliance from rumours and brief quotes in some articles I found in the Oxford University Library, they are an elite group funded by the University to guard the country's most treasured possessions and secrets. But no one knows if they really exist. Well, obviously now *I* do.

I know these things come along once in a lifetime— even then, only if you're lucky. I will finally be able to see the priceless artefacts I teach about every day, some that aren't even known to be in existence anymore. I'll be able to hold them, to study them; it means everything to me.

And you have to be *really* special to get in. Which makes this meeting the most important event of my entire life thus far. Because if an elite alliance thinks you're special, that's your one chance. Your one chance in life to take that big step to be something great.

"Deacon stood behind her naked body wrapped in the rumpled sheet. As she fell back into the embrace of his arms, they gazed at the rolling hills together, both mesmerized by the beauty of the land."

"Are you even allowed to listen to this when you have a customer?" I yell.

"I'm self-employed." Griffin shrugs.

Swallowing my retort I sit back and drum my fingers on my leg. "We are going to make it, right? I mean, you said you could get me there on time."

"Miss, if anyone is going to be able to get you there, it's me."

"That's very evasive. What does that mean?" I try and catch Griffin's eyes in the rear-view mirror.

"It means I can't move the traffic. If it moves, so will you," he says as though it is that simple. "This is why I always tell my customers to leave fifteen minutes earlier than they usually would."

"She shouted with passion the words she had been longing to say, "Wait for me!""

"Turn it off! I can't think straight with that stuff on!" I press my hands to my ears.

"Is this stuff having an emotional effect on you?" Griffin asks, reaching for his notepad. "I keep telling my agent it's too much, but maybe…"

"Ughh!"

"June has always been a bit skittish when it comes to the

thought of romance," the Professor pipes up from beside me.

I look at the Professor, whose eyes seem clear in this moment, and I question what I've done in life to deserve a moment of his clarity at this *exact* moment.

"I wonder why that is," I raise my eyebrow in his direction, forcing all the sarcasm I can muster into my voice.

"Not a clue," he says with genuine puzzlement. "You could be asexual."

"Like a nun?" Griffin asks from the front seat.

"No I'm–" I start in outrage.

"No, nuns are *celibate*, which is a choice to repress your sexual desires and orientation based on your moral or religious beliefs," the Professor explains. "June Bug here just doesn't feel anything for the opposite sex. Or her own sex for that matter."

"I'm not asexual," I say through gritted teeth. "Nor am I gay!"

"Is that possible?" Griffin asks looking over his shoulder, and I see now that he has blue eyes, though they are much darker than the Professor's. "To not feel anything?"

"Quite, my boy," the Professor says. "I believe it dates back to the Two-Spirits tribe, who had gender confusing roles, where both the women and men took on equal tasks. Some speculate it was to conceal the lack of sexual desire on some of the men's part."

21

"Fascinating," Griffin nods from the front seat, writing in his notepad what he's just heard. "That could be interesting material."

"Though, June, you don't have any relation to the Two-Tribes on your father's side. At least none that I know of. Maybe through your late aunt on your grandmother's side..." The Professor reaches for his notebook to jot something down. "I could have a quick look when we get back. Not that it is necessarily a hereditary thing, but always nice to fit a piece in the puzzle."

I look into the rear-view mirror and stare at my reflection.

This is my life.

"Could be worse," Griffin says from the front seat, meeting my eyes in the mirror.

"Could it?" I ask, but before I can dwell on my life I see movement in front of us. "It's moving! The van is moving!"

As the van finally clears out of the street and parks in the driveway just past the church Griffin drives up the side, and once we are into mainstream traffic again things seem to be moving at a good pace.

It's going to be so very close. I look at my watch and see the little hand tick away, as though completely unaware that I desperately need it to slow down.

Chapter Three

"Speak of the devil."

I take my identification back from the security guard who let me in the Ashmolean, and turn my head at the sound of Charles's voice.

"Thank you, Robbie. I think you can go on your break now. We aren't expecting anyone else in the immediate future, though some members of the press should be here in a few hours," Charles addresses the guard before turning to me with one of his dazzling smiles, perfectly set off by his beautifully fitted suit.

Maybe I should have thought a little bit more about my outfit.

Charles always looks ready for the cameras. He styles his hair back and God only knows how he gets that much volume without looking like he dumped a can of mousse on his head. I really should have a word with him about that one day. He has it all: looks, charisma, and more money than he knows what to do with. I think if he weren't my closest friend it would be very hard for me not to hate him.

He comes towards me, putting his hands on my

shoulders while leaning forward, pretending to kiss my cheek.

"Where the bloody hell have you been? You practically beg me to get you a shot with the Alliance and then you're a quarter of an hour late?" he hisses in my ear, and I can't help but stare at his purple polka-dotted bowtie. Before I even have a chance to respond he leans away and turns so his arm is wrapped around my shoulder, pointing me to the others in the room.

I don't even bother taking offense at his words because this is just typical Charles. He's my best friend, or maybe my worst enemy. Sometimes it's hard to tell.

Looking at the people standing in the atrium watching us, I can't help but wonder about Charles's judgment. I know who they all are. One of my qualifying tests for the Alliance was to look over the other potential applicant's CVs and see if I could spot any discrepancies. There were about twenty applicants all together, and the three people standing here must be the chosen ones.

They definitely wouldn't have been my pick of the litter. But who knows, maybe there are things that weren't in their files, things I don't know about, that make them worthy of the honour. Or maybe they're the only ones who were able to pass the entry tests.

Instantly my eyes take them in, locking their features into my memory. It's surprising how misleading a picture can be, which I would never admit out loud, but herein lies the weakness in my own abilities. Pictures can be doctored, items added or taken away. I can identify what they are, commit them to memory, but if the actual picture or information is false then I'm not much use to anyone. Naturally I didn't bring that up during the recruitment process.

"This is Ciara Burk," Charles says as Ciara extends her hand to me.

Ciara's flaming red hair is even more pronounced than it was in her pictures. She keeps it short, the curls shooting out every which way. Her face is covered in a smattering of freckles. She seems softer than I would have thought, almost a little pudgy. Her file was the trickiest out of them all because she seems to be a walking contradiction. She's wearing a black lace dress that is just a little too tight for her in the wrong places and a pink flower brooch. As she walks down the street I bet no one would guess that she is a master in Capoeira, a martial art born in the slave ghettos of Brazil. Her only file discrepancy is she said she's never left Europe, yet her particular skill set would have forced her to travel to South America. Also, she says she doesn't like sweet things, which I now think she lied about. I hope I didn't get marks taken off for that.

"Lovely ta finally meet ya, June," she says, her Irish accent as thick as can be. "Charles here was just singin' yer praises."

Charles smiles at her, but from the tightness around his

eyes I can tell he may have been singing those praises as a distraction tactic.

"Yer dress is just lovely, as well." She self-consciously adjusts her own.

"It's nice to meet you as well, Ciara." I leave it at that because I'm not sure if Ciara or the others are aware of how much I know about them. Taking her hand I'm surprised at the lack of grip she has, especially since I know she could snap me in two if she wanted to.

"Max Lauries." The man standing behind her is ready for my handshake next. Max is the epitome of what I imagined a computer wizard to look like: short, unruly brown hair that flips up at the sides where it hits his ears, rimless spectacles and a dress shirt that has clearly never seen an iron. I know that he can easily clear out my pension in the click of a mouse, though, so I offer him a very wide smile.

"A pleasure," I say, taking his hand.

"The pleasure is all mine," he replies, his hand shaking a little as it grasps mine.

"And finally, Tobias Grant, this is June Jenson," Charles says. I turn to look at the man with the short, cropped hair who is leaning against the doorframe. He doesn't move except to nod in my direction, so I just nod back. I knew he would be the moody one of the bunch. The MI5 agents are always the ones with the hidden woes, aren't they? His file is impeccable, and not a single blemish on his career. Except… I do know that his main assignment was protecting a dignitary's son and wife, taking them to school and to the shopping centre… so what does he have to be moody about?

"All right, now that everyone is here, if you will just follow me," Charles turns around and walks toward the stairs. Ciara quickly falls into step beside him and I end up stepping in line with Max, leaving Tobias to take up the rear.

Recently renovated, the Ashmolean appears old and worldly on the outside, with its grey stone bricks and matching columns lining the entryway. Inside, however, you feel modernity at its best. The polished marble flooring in the centre atrium with winding staircases leading to the exhibits on the upper floors, the old banisters replaced with sleek glass, providing a more open feeling to the building. But with bending staircases and statues placed throughout the pathways, it still retains some old world charm.

"Don't worry about being late," Max says, lowering his voice to me. "I only got here a few moments before you. They didn't give much time with that phone call, did they?"

I smile at him, shaking my head in agreement.

"So, you have the photographic memory, right?"

"Eidetic memory, actually," I say, grasping the banister rail as we start climbing to the second floor. "There's technically no such thing as photographic memory."

"But you can remember whatever you see or read?" he asks, and I can hear the excitement in his tone.

"Most things," I answer, "though usually it depends how good of a look I get. A few seconds and I will retain a general idea. A minute or so of studying something and it's etched in there for life."

"Fascinating," Max replies, and we turn the corner to go up the next flight of stairs.

We pass the entrance to the Ancient Worlds exhibit; I took my students on a tour of this exhibit only a week ago after finishing a teaching series on Tutankhamen.

"You know, I took a few of your classes at Oxford," Max says. "When you were your grandfather's assistant, actually, so I suppose they were technically his classes. Though, I always enjoyed when you took the lectern."

"You studied Ancient Artefacts?" I'm puzzled– this wasn't in his file. I study his face, concerned that I don't remember him. With all the students over the years, it really tests my memory with their faces; some classes were close to two hundred pupils. My classes are not even a quarter of the size of the crowd the Professor used to bring in, not to say that I'm not well sought after in my field of expertise. It's just hard for anyone to stand next to the Professor and shine given his experience and vast knowledge.

"Sadly, no, it was more a matter of me having to take some social courses as well as my computer engineering courses to 'round out my education', as they say. I actually tried my hand at acting first for my elective but they quickly sent me packing," he smiles at the memory. "But I count myself lucky in the end because I enjoyed your class more than I thought I would. My grandfather was greatly interested in Ancient Artefacts; he was always digging holes all over our property, hoping to uncover some hidden treasure. He always admired your grandfather, even after... well... he always thought your grandfather to be a fascinating man."

"I'm glad," I say, trying to remain calm and accept the well-meaning words. "That must have been a while ago; my grandfather hasn't taught for years."

"About five, I believe," Max nods. "I found it interesting, but you didn't manage to convert me, I'm afraid. Computers were always my calling. My grandfather could never wrap his mind around technology, though, so I was appreciative of the knowledge I gained from your grandfather's course. The lectures gave me plenty of material for our evening dinners while my grandfather was still well, so I'm eternally grateful to you."

"Just one more flight," Charles says over his shoulder.

"Where do you think he is taking us?" Max asks, looking around at the different artwork hanging on the walls. "Do you think it will be another test?"

"I have no clue," I shrug. "At this point I just don't know what to expect anymore."

My first test for the Alliance was strenuous. At first I thought the group might be military-based, judging by the activities they made me do. They showed me a map that I got to study for twenty seconds before they blindfolded me and drove me to... well, I'm still not too sure where I was...

but I was surrounded by forest. I was pushed out of the car, blindfold removed, and told I had four hours to make it to the 'X' I had briefly glimpsed on the map.

That was the scariest four hours of my life. I have my PhD in Ancient History, and there I was, running through the forest, out of my mind with worry that some sort of snake might jump out at me.

But I made it– in three hours, actually. I don't think they expected me to run in a complete state of panic the whole time.

For the next test I had to sit on the London Underground, on the Piccadilly Line, in the middle cart, facing the door. At every stop they hung a poster that I briefly glimpsed as the doors opened and people filed in and out. At the end of the fifty-three stops there was a man waiting for me in an orange coat with an envelope. I was told to go to the toilets, answer the questions about the posters, and return within ten minutes.

My final test was the personnel files.

All of this over the course of six months, and not once did they contact me to say how I'd done or that they would be in contact again. Each time I went home and thought I'd botched the whole thing up. Then a few weeks later, out of the blue, I would get a phone call with the location of my next test.

"I couldn't believe it when they first contacted me," Max says as we climb the last few steps. "I thought someone was having a laugh, but when I tried to trace the email I knew it was the real thing."

"This is it," Charles stops outside of a set of black double doors. Looking down the hallway, there is nothing to distinguish this door from any other. "Through these doors the Ashmolean holds their special viewing galleries."

Max looks at me to see if I've got a clue, but I meet his eyes and shrug.

"Shall we?" Charles asks this to no one in particular, and must not expect an answer, for he swipes an electronic card through the machine fastened to the door and pushes both the doors open. We file in quietly behind him.

As soon as we enter I look around the room, my eyes widening at the sheer sight and I can't help the gasp that escapes from my lips.

As I survey the room my heart hammers in my chest, the clammy feeling on my hands quickly travelling up my arms to my face and I have to tell myself to calm down.

All around the room are countless artefacts that I immediately recognize as pieces I've admired from afar for so many years, pieces that my grandfather has spoken of since I was born. Swords with gilded handles, far exceeding any workmanship that has been created for centuries, with thick, iron bonded sheaths. Dull silver filling every corner of the room, the display lights expertly placed to accentuate the collection of emeralds, rubies, garnets, and the other precious gemstones embedded in the pieces.

Most small articles are sheltered under the protective glass, though some armour and weaponry exhibits are protected simply with heavy rope guards.

"This room has been specially designed and climate controlled. Each case has its own alarm, and can only be unlocked from a remote location," Charles explains to the group.

My body naturally gravitates to the display case in front of me; when my hand goes forward I notice it trembling and pull it back, not sure if the outer case has a perimeter alarm.

On the table is a variety of gold jewellery. The gold shoulder clasps adorned with garnets are more beautiful than one could ever imagine. My eyes scan the interwoven animals etched throughout the piece and adhere it to memory. To the left is the Great Buckle. The piece is far more intricate than the pictures led me to believe it would be; the chip carving done so meticulously that it is astonishing to think someone crafted this with their own hands.

"What are they doing here?" I turn to ask Charles.

Ignoring my question, he turns to the others in the room. "The security is very tight, of course. The cameras are positioned throughout the room so no angle is left vulnerable. Each exhibit has its own handler, who has brought it in and set it up. They finished a few hours ago, though please be careful because some of the roped off exhibits haven't been bolted to the ground yet. But naturally, security will be extremely vigilant. Never before have this many priceless artefacts been under one roof at the same time."

"Is this... er... unusual then? For this all to be together?" Max asks.

I turn to look at the others, who all have puzzled expressions on their faces, oblivious as to what they are seeing. I also notice I am the only one who has approached the cases, the others are clearly not interested in getting any closer. Standing straighter, I tell myself to be calm. I have nothing to be nervous about.

"These are the artefacts that were discovered at Sutton-Hoo," I explain. "The Anglo-Saxon ship burial ground in Suffolk."

"I remember studyin' that," Ciara nods. "It happened in the forties?"

"The original excavation was commissioned in 1939. The landowner had no clue what was buried in the mounds on her property. The archaeologist, Dr Brown, uncovered a twenty-seven meter long ship; at the ship's centre was a burial chamber filled with more treasures than he could have ever dreamed of: a room filled with silverware, gold jewellery, and most famously, an iron helmet," I point to the helmet which is displayed in the far right corner of the room. "It is still considered one of the greatest archaeological finds of all time."

"So this is all that we have left from the Anglo-Saxons?" Max asks, suddenly taking a greater interest in the artefacts now that he has some context as to what they are.

My eye catches Tobias's, who is watching me intently from the corner of the room. He seems to have moulded into the corner, and I'd almost forgotten he was in the room. His study makes me uncomfortable, as though he is watching for my every reaction, and suddenly the Professor's voice rings crystal clear in my head: *"Why shouldn't I still teach this? My entire career has been spent studying this. I haven't done anything wrong!"* I turn my attention back to the others, remembering to keep my voice as detached as possible as I push the Professor's voice from my mind.

"Unfortunately, we don't have much of the art or metalwork left from the time, with all the plundering of the churches in the eighth and ninth centuries. Besides the material found in the excavations, what we do have left is what the churches were able to preserve. There have been smaller discoveries throughout the years, people finding random pieces buried on their property," I say, looking from Max to Ciara. "Most of the time people have no clue what they possess and pass pieces down as family heirlooms. By the time the true value of the piece is discovered it is usually largely deteriorated from mishandling."

"So, this find is important because no one touched it before Dr Brown?" Ciara asks.

"Yes, there's that. But it's also who is rumoured to be buried in the ship which gives these pieces even more significance."

The information seems to flow from my lips, though my mind tells me it might be better not to say too much. But growing up with these as bedtime stories, the knowledge is second nature to me; the Anglo-Saxons were always the Professor's greatest interest.

"Was it royalty?" Ciara's thick accent takes on a note of excitement. Usually I would be thrilled when someone is this keen to know history; recently I've noticed people are far more interested in the future than the past.

"Yes, it was. With all the extravagant riches found in the ship, it is believed that it is the burial ground for King Raedwald. Most of these pieces have been held in the British Museum of London, but I am assuming they are on loan for your exhibit?" I direct this question to Charles, and he nods.

"For some reason, I thought the pieces would be a bit bigger. You know, when you read and see the pictures about these things in the paper... It's amazing to think this is all we have... considering it represents multiple centuries. There really should be more..." Max looks up at my stricken face and quickly realizes his mistake. "Sorry, I only meant–"

I carefully keep my face averted from Tobias's studying glare.

This is exact reason I have stayed away from these pieces, and not followed in my grandfather's devotion to Anglo-Saxon history. I didn't want to encounter any raised eyebrows from my interest. Of course, the Professor says I raise eyebrows with my *lack* of interest. You would think as an innocent person one would know how to behave.

"Well, thank you for our history lesson, Professor," Charles smiles, obviously noting the uncomfortable feeling that has taken over the room.

Aware of the others studying me, I idly wander over to the Illuminated Manuscript, its gold and silver etches effectively "illuminated" under the light. My eyes run over the miniature illustrations used instead of text to tell the story, in awe of the implications of the piece and how it had educated the illiterate ruling classes of its time.

"Are we ta mind all this?" Ciara asks, astonished as she looks around the room at the vast amount of historical art on display.

"No, these pieces are not your responsibility," Charles assures her, and walks over to a tall display in the centre of the room, currently draped with a black sheet. "This is what you will be guarding."

Once Charles takes the sheet off I instinctively take a step back, trying to create as much distance from it as possible. My back presses against something solid before I hear the sound of metal falling.

"Oh shit! Oh my God, I'm so sorry! My fault," Max apologizes, quickly trying to stand up the metal rope pole he knocked over when I bumped into him.

I turn to look back at the display, my whole body shaking.

"Is that another piece from the museum?" Ciara asks

Charles.

"No, this is a piece that was only recently discovered. No one knew it still existed," Charles says, and I can feel his eyes fixed my face. "It was anonymously donated about a month ago to the Ashmolean."

"It's terribly important?" Ciara says, looking from Charles to me.

"Terribly," Charles tells her. "This, ladies and gentlemen, is the Shield of Quell."

"It's the missing piece from Sutton-Hoo," I manage to breathe out.

Chapter Four

Max is still trying to fix the display I had a hand in knocking over, but I ignore him and instead walk towards the Shield.

If examining its veracity I would say it's the right size, about two feet in diameter, a perfect circle. The Shield itself is made from wood, which I can see has deteriorated, but not to the extent that it would have to be replaced; thus making it even more invaluable. Most likely lime or alder, popular choices for that time because it didn't split like oak and other woods. It must have been wrapped well. Although not in mint condition, I've definitely seen far worse damage to less significant relics, and the fact that it is still in one piece is a testament to those who preserved it. The dark leather material covering most of the middle section is tarnished at the ends, either from wear during battle or acquired during the interim. On the tattered edges is impeccable ink work, styled in a pattern not so different from the Great Buckle. But all these details pale in comparison to the beautiful metalwork of the Shield's boss: the palm-sized circle at the centre is made completely of gold, the metal housing grape-like clusters of rubies.

"The Gala is in two days. We've made an announcement that there is a new piece, but beyond that the public is unaware of what this is, and the Ashmolean would like to keep it that way. A select amount of journalists are due to arrive here in an hour to take some pictures of the closed doors and to take my statement, but they too will not be privy to what we have acquired. The suspense will be sure to drum up a lot of new attention and financial support for the museum. I believe the museum is going for the shock factor; it seems people are more willing to reach into their pockets to contribute if they're caught off guard," Charles says, laughing at his own amusing observation. "The guest list has been kept to a minimum, and unbeknownst to them there has been a thorough background check done on each guest."

"You are all here because you can offer a unique skill set to the Alliance," Charles says, looking at us one by one.

"Max, you will be in charge of the guest list. Each guest will be given an electronic identification card that is to be scanned as they go in and out of the building. I don't believe I need to mention that nothing should be able to be duplicated or altered?" At Charles's raised eyebrow Max nervously nods in agreement. "You are also in charge of this case and its security alarms. If someone breathes too close to it, I want an alarm waking up the neighbourhood."

"Consider it done," Max says, stepping closer to the glass that protects the Shield, inspecting the seams.

"Ciara, you are going to be circulating the party. You are quick, and if anyone gets out of hand I'm sure you can control the situation without making a scene?"

Ciara nods, "I'm quite good at steering people in the right direction."

"Tobias, other areas of the museum will be open during the Gala, but this room will have a maximum occupancy of twenty people at one time. You will need to control the flow, as well be a standing deterrent for anyone who may even be contemplating getting too close to the Shield or the other artefacts. I'm hoping you can get the job done while being somewhat tactful?"

Tobias lets out a small grunt, looking around the room to survey its weaknesses.

Charles nods his approval at the group, his eyes falling back to the Shield.

The admiration in his eyes as he surveys the treasure sets off a spark inside of me. How long has he known that this piece was in existence, and that it would be donated to the Ashmolean? How could he keep this a secret from me? He knows the full extent of what happened with the Professor; what it did to him, to his career. What it did to me.

"And me?" I ask pointedly.

Charles looks at me as though I'm something he isn't quite sure how to deal with. I've seen that look before, it's the same expression he has when he approaches the Professor, unsure of what kind of day it will be.

"June, for this particular assignment you will be here for historical significance on the piece. Naturally we have had experts verify the Shield, but people are bound to have questions. There is very little knowledge of its original origin and I'm relying on you to educate our guests. No one knows more about the Anglo-Saxon time period– well, besides your grandfather, but clearly–"

At his abrupt stop, I dart my eyes to Tobias, who watches the exchange closely.

I must stop doing this; Tobias must think I am guilty, looking to him like that every time my grandfather's name is mentioned. The trouble is, out of the entire group he is the one that intimidates me the most.

"Anyways, you're the best for the job," Charles nods at the others, probably hoping to get a little enthusiasm out of them.

Deciding not to respond, I stare at Charles to see if he likes being put on the spot as much as I've enjoyed it since I arrived.

Charles looks at me, offering me a tight smile. "Perhaps we should have a word? Outside," he adds.

I try to offer him a similar smile in return but with the others watching the exchange, I feel it falter. "Of course."

"We should only be a moment," Charles nods to Tobias, and I wonder if he is somehow indicating to Tobias to keep an ear out in case I create a scene.

Which is quite possible at this exact moment.

Placing his hand on my lower back, Charles leads me out of the room and turns right down the corridor. At the end he turns left and keeps walking until we hit a dead end.

"Okay, before you go off on me—" Charles begins.

"Are you *insane*? How could you do this to me?" I cry out, stepping away from his grasp.

"I'm trying to *help* you—"

"Help me? How? By ruining what is left of the Professor's reputation? Ruining mine by association?" I shake my head at how thick Charles can be sometimes. "Oh God, Charles, what have you done?"

"What I've done is finally get you and your grandfather's names out of the *dirt*," he raises his voice on the last word, and it echoes in the empty hallway. He takes a breath and calms himself before continuing. "The Shield clears your name, for Christ's sake!"

I can't help the laugh that escapes from my throat. "If you really believe that, you're even stupider than I thought."

"I will choose to believe that the shock of the moment is inhibiting you from seeing reason right now. The Shield has been found, June. It in no way traces back to your grandfather. This is *good* news."

"No," I shake my head. "All that shield does is prove that there was something in that burial tomb twenty years ago!"

"Are you not listening?" Charles says, reaching his hands towards me. "Your grandfather said there was nothing in that tomb. This proves he was right!"

"*How*? Because he wasn't the one that donated it?" I ask.

"Exactly," Charles says, in exasperation.

Sometimes it shocks me how a highly educated man like Charles can be this oblivious to reality. I can tell he believes every word he says, and it infuriates me, but also takes the edge off of my anger, considering his misguided intentions seem to be somewhat honourable.

"Well, who did then?" I ask. "Who discovered the Shield?"

At Charles's hesitation, I throw my arms in the air.

"You don't have a clue, do you?" I start to walk back and forth in short strides down the corridor, trying to think through all the implications. The Professor won't survive this again: the scandal, the accusations. I can only imagine the headlines, how the reporters will spin it: *Professor who forgets everything finally remembers where he's put lost treasure from Sutton-Hoo.*

"The benefactor wanted to remain anonymous; they contacted me through email, everything was very secretive," Charles runs a hand through his hair, the other hand resting on his hip, his suit jacket falling open. "Max is trying to go back through the system– or whatever it is you do– to try and figure out who this guy is, but with no luck so far. But none of that even matters. Don't you see? Your grandfather doesn't even know how to turn on a computer. I barely do!"

"That is a loose argument at best," I say, shaking my

head.

Some mysterious benefactor who contacted Charles by email donated the Shield. It's true the Professor doesn't know how to use a computer; we don't even have one in the house. But in this day and age that means nothing. What if he's accused of selling the treasure– and his buyer is the one who made the anonymous donation? I'm shaking at the thought of even bringing any of this up with the Professor– anytime the Shield comes up in conversation he flies into an immediate rage.

"Why couldn't you tell me? Why would you do this to me?"

Maybe if I had been prepared, I could have spoken to the Professor about it. Somehow broached the subject over time. The Shield will be revealed in two days; an impossibly short time to try and get him to cope with this. How am *I* going to cope with this? And to think of what the others are thinking about me right now, what they will think of me when they understand the implications of the Shield.

"I couldn't tell you because I needed you to react the exact way that you did," Charles says, grabbing my shoulders to stop my pacing. "You now have three eyewitnesses who can testify that you had absolutely no idea that the Shield of Quell had been located. Hell, from the look on your face, I would swear you didn't even think it *existed!*"

"I didn't," I voice in disbelief. "This whole time, I thought those reporters were crazy. Preying on an old man who was starting to forget everything that he held dear for the sake of their news stories. They searched our home, his office. The Professor was down in that tomb for only a few minutes before Dr Cooke climbed in after him. How would he have removed it without anyone seeing?"

The old arguments roll off my tongue. I know them by heart; I can hear the Professor repeat them over and over to me. It's been on a loop in my mind for a quarter of my life.

"And this proves it," Charles says, his voice trying to coax some encouragement from me. "Someone must have been in that tomb before your grandfather even got there. Someone removed the Shield. They probably didn't even think anyone would notice it was ever there."

I nod at his words. They sound good, so very appealing. What he says makes sense, but somehow nothing about this seems right.

"Is this why I was asked to be a part of the Alliance?" I ask, the thought suddenly popping into my mind amidst all the worry. It sounds crazy, probably even irrational, but I feel cheated. I feel stupid. I'd worked so hard on those tests, putting my best foot forward, doing all I could to ensure that I would be an asset to their organization. But I wanted to be an asset because of my talents and abilities, not because of whom I happen to be related to.

Charles thinks about it, obviously deciding on the best way to answer. He looks around to make sure no one is listening before leaning even closer to me. "I was contacted by the Alliance a year ago. All I was told was that there was a priceless artefact that was going to be on loan to the museum. They knew I worked for the museum, knew of my family connections from the very beginning. I was told to begin recruiting individuals to guard this secret artefact. It was *days* after that when you happened to see the Alliance files on my desk."

I process his admission, thinking it through. "So you had no clue when you originally mentioned my name to the Alliance that we would be guarding the Shield?"

"Of course not. I didn't even know what we were guarding until a few days ago, just that the person donating the artefact was insistent on securing the Alliance to guard it. I thought the donor was just being paranoid– this museum is filled with artefacts– but now knowing what it is, I can understand why they want to err on the side of caution," Charles says.

I shake my head because I can't help but believe him. Only Charles would be asked by a secret alliance to recruit people to guard priceless artefacts and not ask any questions.

"Does the Alliance know my connection with all of this now?" I ask. I already know the answer, but I think it's important to see just how obtuse Charles is in this whole situation.

"That's the best part," Charles smiles, and I can see he is finally starting to relax under the impression that I seem to be coming around to the whole idea. "When I first mentioned your name to them and told them what you are able to do, they were fully on board. Before the connection between the Shield and your grandfather had even been made!"

I close my eyes and exhale. Poor Charles. It must be nice to be that naïve.

"Charles, they knew what was going to be guarded. Please try and think this through," I plead, pinching my forehead with my fingers.

"I *have* thought it through," Charles says, finally reaching his breaking point. "I think *you* need to think this through. This is an out for you; a once in a lifetime opportunity. There are going to be reporters here in an hour, from the same newspapers that have accused your grandfather from the beginning. So, we can both get behind this and be an active part in clearing your family name, or you can sit on the side-lines and give everyone that little inkling of doubt to hold on to."

Shaking his head at my lack of response, Charles brushes past me.

"Wait!" I say, and he stops walking. "What are you getting out of all of this? Because I know this isn't all about clearing my name."

Taking a deep breath, he slowly turns back to look at me. "If all goes well, I'll take over as Curator for the Ashmolean."

I close my eyes. Of course he will.

"Charles, I don't think you see—"

A sudden loud wail stops my thoughts, and we both look in the direction we just came from.

"What the hell?"

We both half run, half walk back to the room we left the others in just minutes before.

"Argh!" The yell greets me as I walk through the door. "Take your bloody hands off me!"

In his underpants and shirt, Ciara holds the Professor in a headlock, his arms flailing about at his side. Of course he's not wearing any bloody trousers. Again.

"One wrong move," she warns him, moving her hands up ever so slightly.

"Professor!" I say, running over to him.

"Here she is! I told you she was in here!" he yells to no one in particular. "She's here to introduce me, you bloody idiot! This meeting is for *me*."

"He says he knows ya, June," Ciara says, not relaxing her grip on the Professor's head in the slightest.

"He's my grandfather!" I yell, trying to pry her fingers off him "Let go!"

"He was trying to get at the Shield," Tobias says from behind me. I jump at the sound of his voice, realizing it's the first time he has spoken since we've met. His voice is much higher than I imagined it would be, almost child-like. Maybe that's why he is the silent type.

"He's not well," I say, and look to Charles for help.

"Ciara, please let him go," Charles says, but doesn't get

any closer to the action than the door.

"Sorry June, we just couldn't take a chance," Ciara says, releasing the Professor and then attempting to pull the hem of her skirt down.

"Where's Max? He knows that he is my grandfather," I say, looking around the room. "How did he even get in here?"

"I was patrolling the corridors," Tobias says, pointing in the direction we just came as an excuse for his absence.

"I was studying that ruddy helmet," Ciara says, shaking her head. "Never in me life have I not heard someone sneak up on me like that. Yer grandpappy must have the feet of a puma."

And this is who Charles picked to join the prestigious Alliance.

"Max has gone to talk to the front guard about their current security software system," Tobias explains. "He's getting ready to activate the alarm for the display case but needs some more information."

"June, have you seen what they've got here?" the Professor half yells, staggering over to the display of the Shield, rubbing his neck. "A bloody joke, that's what it is."

"Professor, please," I say, trying to restrain him from getting too close. I widen my legs in front of his body, trying to block his sickeningly pale legs from the view of the others.

"If they are trying to pass this off as what I think they are, they'll be the laughing stock of this bloody university in no time– it might actually be a nice break," he says, leaning closer to the display and chuckling. "The detailing is immaculate but there's no way the wood would have survived! It would have had to be kept in impeccable conditions–"

"We've had it authenticated, Professor Jenson," Charles comes to stand beside us, his eyes locked on the Shield.

"Bogwash," the Professor waves him off. "You've wasted your money on some bloody scam artist here. I'm telling you, this is not the Shield!"

"I assure you, it was authenticated by the best," Charles says, and I close my eyes at his words, preparing myself for the backlash.

"The cheek!" the Professor spits out. "*I* am the best! It's that bloody Daniel, isn't it? You've asked him to authenticate it, haven't you?"

Charles averts his eyes from the Professor's, which could be his way of trying to end the conversation, but the Professor takes it as an admission of guilt.

"Well, it doesn't matter, because he's lied to you! The leading Anglo-Saxon historian in the country has never seen this before, so how in the world could you have had it authenticated?"

The Professor takes a step back and loses his balance, but my arm reaches to steady him.

"You hear that? I've never seen this bloody thing before in my life!" he yells in the direction of Ciara before turning his eyes to my face. "June Bug, be a dear and fetch me something cool to drink. I think I'm done for the day."

Before I can stop him, he lowers himself onto the platform. Watching in what feels like slow motion, I see the display holding the Illuminated Manuscript fall backwards; it hits the ground with a thud and sirens begin to wail.

"Oh for fuck's sake," Charles says, throwing his hand to his hair. Unconcerned with the Professor, who is on his back with his legs in the air, Charles leaps over him and tries to pick the Manuscript's heavy display case back up. "I said the displays weren't bolted and to be careful— now look at what's happened! Tobias, help me!"

Tobias rushes past as I finally get the Professor back on his feet.

"Ciara, go down and find Max. Tell him to turn these bloody alarms off!" Charles yells over the sirens, the Manuscript's stand still lying on the ground. Charles's eyes scan the piece, sweat visible on his forehead. "I don't think it's damaged."

"I can help—"

"No!" Charles says, holding his hand up to stop me from coming any closer. "Just get him out of here!"

"Charles, I'm sorry. He's not well."

The Professor is looking around the room, obviously confused as to where he is and where the loud noise is coming from.

"Just go!" he orders.

Nodding, I take the Professor by the elbow, turning him towards the door.

"Did I do this?" he looks towards the sound before returning his eyes to my face.

"No, Professor," I say, propelling him to the door. "You haven't done anything."

Chapter Five

I hit the final step when the alarm stops ringing. I wrap my arms around the Professor to help guide him the last few steps. The security guard who let me in when I first arrived is sitting at the desk with the phone to his ear, watching us in bewilderment before he stands up.

"Charles told me to let you know that they were just testing out the system," I say as I pass his desk, offering him a hurried smile. "Must have given you a right headache."

"Bit chilly tonight," the Professor says, crossing his arms across his chest.

When I pull the handle of the front door it doesn't budge, and I turn to the security guard who stares at the Professor's underpants.

I raise my eyebrows while clearing my throat.

"The door?"

He finally pulls his eyes from the Christmas briefs and springs into action.

"Er– yes– sorry. I was just calling about the alarm," he says. He leans across his desk to press the door release button on the wall. "Will you– umm– be returning, Miss Jenson?"

"I think they sell whiskey in the gift shop," the Professor says, looking over my shoulder, searching for the sign past the atrium.

"Not tonight, thanks," I say, opening the door and directing the Professor out.

As the Professor and I exit the Ashmolean I see Griffin pacing in front of the car parked at the curb. When he sees the Professor he throws his hands in the air.

"Oh thank God! He's with you," Griffin says, walking towards us while wiping pretend sweat from his forehead.

"What the hell happened?" I say, stopping a few feet away from him. "You were supposed to be watching him!"

"I know," he says. He looks slightly guilty as he tries to apologize. "We went to get some whiskey but the shops were closed, so I thought I'd just bring him back here and wait for you."

"So you let him wander into the museum?" I ask.

I tell myself to keep calm.

"I didn't *let* him do anything," Griffin shakes his head. "He was in the backseat sleeping, and my book ended so I went into the boot to get the next one."

He holds up the CD for me to see.

"And you didn't notice him get out?" I yell.

"Didn't hear a peep," Griffin says in wonderment. "That man has pretty light feet."

"Argh!" I scream, taking a step closer. "You are fired!"

"What?" he asks frowning. "Why?"

"Are you seriously asking me that? Let me try to explain this so that tiny little brain of yours can comprehend it," I say, grabbing the CD out of his hand. "Maybe because an old man with dementia, who you were supposed to be minding, managed to take off his pants, wander right past you and go into the museum where he nearly destroyed centuries old and priceless artefacts, all while you were searching for the next cheap romance on tape!"

"But he didn't destroy them."

"What?" I ask, leaning closer, unsure if I heard him correctly.

"You said he *nearly* destroyed them, so that means they're fine, right?" he shrugs his shoulders. "What's the problem?"

I stare at his face, wondering if he is being serious.

"The problem is—" before I am able to continue the sharp ringtone of my phone pierces the air. Ignoring Griffin's confused face, I zip open my bag and grab my phone.

"Hello?" I say, bringing it to my ear.

"June, it's Charles," he whispers over the line.

"Charles?" I push the phone closer to my ear. "I can barely hear you, what's—"

"June, listen to me," he cuts me off. "The Shield is gone."

"*What?*"

"June, I can't help you unless you are honest with me. Listen, I'll meet you outside, just give me the Shield and no one has to know." I can hear the sheer panic in Charles's voice.

"Are you *crazy*? I didn't take the Shield!" I say, looking around frantically as though it might be outside the Ashmolean somewhere. "What do you mean it's missing?"

"Tobias and I managed to get the Illuminated Manuscript back in place. Ciara still wasn't back so we went to search for her, and Max left to turn off the alarm. When we got back— June, the Shield is *gone*."

It sounds like Charles is nearly in tears.

"Oh fuck, this is bad. This is really, *really* bad," I can hear Charles's voice shake. "Christ, the reporters are going to be here any minute!"

"I'm coming back in," I say, turning around.

"No!" Charles yells. "June, you swear to me you don't have the Shield?"

"I swear it!"

"Then you need to get out of here. Go home," he orders.

"I can't go home, are you crazy? People will think—"

"What will people think when you are here and it is discovered *missing*? The reporters would have a fucking field day with this! No, it's better if no one knows you were even here," Charles says, and I can hear raised voices joining him in the room.

"Charles, I can't just go home and pretend nothing has happened," I argue.

"We just need a little time," he whispers. "I'll protect you as best I can. Go now! Wait for me to call you."

"I– wait a second," I say. "Is this a test?"

"What?" Charles asks.

The panic inside immediately starts to recede as I begin to figure out what is going on.

"This is a test, isn't it?" I ask. "The Alliance wants to see how I will react when it all hits the fan, don't they? Well I'm not going to show them I run away from a challenge!"

They obviously know who I am; they know who my family is. Bringing me on must have caused some concern, surely.

So that's it. This is all just a giant ruse. The Shield isn't real, it couldn't possibly be! They must have set this whole thing up; my final test to get into the Alliance is a test of my past. It seems a bit much for them to have moved all of those other artefacts from London just for me, but it's actually quite flattering, really. I turn around, ready to go back in the Ashmolean, when Charles's voice cuts through my thoughts.

"June, are you crazy? The police are on their way, this isn't a bloody test," Charles says. "You need to go now!"

"Right, where are the police then?" I challenge.

Suddenly my ears pick up the sirens in the far distance. Wow, they actually called the police. I'm not sure how I feel about that. It's a bit over the top, no?

"June, listen to me. This isn't a test. This isn't some sort of drill," Charles says. "If you are here when the police show up, everyone will assume you did this. Never mind them accusing you, you brought the *Professor* here. He already nearly destroyed one of the artefacts while he was here, do you think it's such a large leap for them to believe he took the Shield as well? He'll surely be arrested! The London Times will have his face on the front page by morning!"

"I– but that's not fair. They have no proof!" I say.

I hear shouting from inside the building, more noise than just Charles, Tobias and Ciara could make. The panic that started to recede before is back in full force. What if this isn't a test?

"And that stopped them last time?" he asks.

"Charles, swear it," I say, my hand shaking as it clutches the phone. "Swear to me that the Shield is gone."

"I swear it," he says. "Get out of here, now."

I hear the click and bring the phone away from my ear so I can stare at it in disbelief.

This cannot be happening. How is it possible that someone stole the Shield? We were there the entire time. *Someone* was there the entire time. This has to be a misunderstanding, some sort of mistake–

The sound of the loud alarm siren blazes again from the museum, and I jump.

But the Shield didn't just wander off on it's own. Something is wrong. I knew this whole thing wasn't right from the beginning.

"What the devil?" the Professor says, turning back

towards the Ashmolean. "Do you think there is a fire? Should we help?"

When the Professor takes a step towards the museum my mind finally clicks into the reality of what potentially is happening here. I may *want* to stay and figure this whole thing out, but Charles is right. The Professor cannot be here when the reporters arrive.

"We need to get him home," I say to Griffin, turning the Professor back towards the car.

"We?" Griffin says, not moving.

"Yes, *we*," I repeat.

I open the back door to the car and hear the distant sound of police sirens competing with the alarm from the museum.

"You know, something tells me— and I'm only basing this off that very disturbing, one-sided conversation I just heard, and the fact that the alarm has gone off in the museum, and the police are on their way— that you need my help right now," Griffin says, slowly leaning against the front passenger side door of the car. He looks up at the museum and watches people run back and forth by the main floor windows.

Where did all of those people come from? I could only see the one main guard in the building the whole time I was in there.

I glare at him as I help the Professor put on his seatbelt.

"Now, I'm the type of guy who is always willing to help

someone in need; I consider it my civic duty," he says, still looking at the Ashmolean, the police sirens growing louder. "But I don't want to overstep my boundaries here. I mean, I am just a taxi driver."

I close the Professor's door with a bang and place my hands on my hips.

"Are you going to drive us or not?"

The sirens seem like they are on top of us.

"Oh, did you want me to drive you?" Griffin says, his tone full of innocence.

"You know I do," I say through clenched teeth.

"Because I'm just not sure, sometimes it's hard for me to think because I have such a small brain," he says, tapping the side of his temple.

"Can you please drive us home?" I say the words slowly, enunciating each syllable.

He studies my face for a moment, watching my unflinching stare. When I see the bright lights from the police cars in the distance, reflecting off of the tall buildings, my left eye twitches slightly, which causes him to grin.

"Of course," he says, smiling while walking to the driver's door. "All you had to do was ask."

Chapter Six

As we drive away from the Ashmolean and make our way onto the motorway I continually look over my shoulder. I'm convinced the police will appear behind us at any moment.

"You know, I think we should just start over," Griffin says from beside me in the front seat. "Let's just forget that you tried to unlawfully sack me— without just cause, might I add— and just chalk it up to experience."

"I unlawfully sacked—" I swallow my retort.

Offering him a tight smile, I look over my shoulder at the Professor, who stares out the window.

"It's a forgery," he says quietly, almost to himself, the internal struggle written on his features. "It has to be."

"Try to rest," I tell him.

We drive for a few more minutes without anyone saying anything, though I can hear the Professor flipping through his journal in the back seat.

"So... do I want to know what is happening here?" Griffin asks, looking in his rear-view mirror to study the Professor.

"No," I shake my head.

"Because I won't understand?" he asks, tilting his head in my direction.

"If you think I'm going to let you off the hook by making me feel bad that I insulted you, you're wrong," I say, crossing my arms across my chest.

Griffin doesn't respond, which brings the car to complete silence again. I notice he hasn't put his new CD in either, even though I threw it at him when he got in the car.

"You know, I'm actually a pretty smart guy," he says, and I can hear the defensive note in his voice. "I went to Cambridge."

I raise my eyebrows in his direction.

"Alright, I went to Leeds," he admits. "But I graduated, and not at the bottom, either."

I nod and hope he will be satisfied with that. Really, I don't have the time to stroke his ego while running for my life.

"This taxi driving thing is only temporary, you know, until I'm able to sell one of my plays," he says. "Any day now."

"I don't think you are stupid," I acknowledge, though I'm not sure why I am putting him out of his misery, considering I might be arrested soon because of him. "Believe it or not, I'm actually doing you a favour. The less you know, the less you will have to testify to in court."

He lets out a low whistle. "That bad, huh?"

I check my phone, willing it to ring. Willing all this to be one big mistake. Why has Charles not called?

"A watched pot never boils," Griffin idly mutters.

Because I can see him watching me I put the phone down in my lap so the screen is pointing away from his face, but I make sure I can still see it.

"Daniel has put them up to this, that rat bastard," the Professor says, getting agitated again in the back seat. "It wasn't down there! There was nothing there!"

"I know, Professor," I say, turning in my seat. "We will get it sorted. It will be fine, no one thinks you stole it."

"They all think I stole it!" he yells, his closed fist coming up to his mouth on the soft sob that escapes.

I'm not sure if he is referring to what happened at the Ashmolean or what happened all those years ago.

His head jerks back at the sound of his own sob and I see his eyes go distant before a frown creases his forehead. "Did we get the whiskey?" he asks, looking around on the floor of the backseat. "We went to the shops. The young chap took me there."

"We're on our way now, sir," Griffin says from the front seat, nodding. The promise seems to mollify the Professor for now and he sinks back in his seat.

A few minutes later I hear him lightly snoring. I shuffle in my seat, my agitated state making a comfortable position impossible.

"So... he stole something?" Griffin asks, making sure to

keep his voice lowered while tipping his head in the Professor's direction.

"No!" I say, but when the Professor stirs I lower my voice. "It's just a misunderstanding."

"Right," Griffin nods. "A misunderstanding... so you're fleeing the scene."

"We weren't fleeing the scene; you don't know anything about this." I narrow my eyes. "My grandfather didn't steal anything. They'll find the Shield; this is all just a huge mistake."

"A shield?" Griffin raises his eyebrow. "That's a pretty big thing to misplace."

He's right of course, though I would never admit this out loud to him. Where could it be? How do you lose a nearly two thousand year old shield? It's not like someone put it down somewhere and forgot about it, it was in that secured case. Someone must have stolen it, there's no other explanation for it. But who?

The first artefact the Alliance was commissioned with and we lost it within the hour. But there has to be something to prove what happened. Charles had said there was security for the other pieces, surely the system's cameras picked something up, and something there will identify the thieves. That's probably exactly what Charles has them working on now. He wanted me to leave so they wouldn't be distracted with the wrong person and would therefore be able to focus on finding the real thief. He'll call in a minute. We might even be able to have a laugh about this one day.

Well, he'll laugh, I'll probably still break out into a cold sweat at the thought.

"They'll find it," I say, more to reassure myself.

"Maybe the Professor's right. Maybe that Daniel he was muttering about did it," Griffin suggests.

I shake my head. "He wasn't even there. The Professor is confused."

"He's not the only one," Griffin mutters, merging onto the next road. "So what happens? If they don't find it. I mean."

"I don't know." I bring my fingernail to my lip and start to bite.

What happens when people steal priceless artefacts? Obviously we didn't do it, but as Charles pointed out, that never stopped the public from nearly lynching the Professor the last time. Surely they won't let him walk away from this again, proof or no proof.

We make the rest of the journey in silence, my mobile not ringing, not even a text from Charles to alert me as to what is going on. My fingers itch to type him a quick message, but my mind tells me it is important to keep distance. Let Charles handle this. No one besides the four know I was even there— and that bloody security guard; I'm sure he won't forget the Professor's underpants anytime soon.

When we arrive I climb out of the car and open the

Professor's door, the sound causing him to startle awake.

"We're home," I tell him, putting a reassuring hand on his shoulder as I help him out of the car.

"Lovely brisk evening," he says once he's standing on the front lawn. "I think I'll run in and put the kettle on."

Leaning into the back of the car I retrieve the Professor's trousers and umbrella before turning to see him walk through the front door. The plant where I keep a spare key hidden is tipped over, the soil spilling out. The Professor obviously couldn't wait the two minutes it would have taken me to get my own key out of my purse and open the door.

I close the car door before turning to look at Griffin, who leans on the driver's side door with his elbow resting on the roof.

"Thank you for the ride," I offer, hugging the trousers closer to my chest.

"Will you be alright?" he asks, pointing to the open front door.

"We'll be fine," I say, attempting to reassure both of us.

"Well, give me a ring, if you ever need a ride," he says, offering me a lopsided grin. "I'm known to drive a mean getaway car."

Despite my best efforts a small smile lifts up the side of my mouth.

"June!" The Professor yells from the front door, the kettle in his left hand with the cord swinging like a pendulum. "Where are the bloody teabags?"

"I better just…" I say pointing to the Professor.

"Of course," Griffin nods. "Goodnight Professor!"

The Professor looks at him, seeming to decide whether he knows him or not, and lifts one shoulder to wave. He retreats back into the house, me following on his heels.

Chapter Seven

Sitting down at the vanity table in my room, I look into the mirror and sigh. The antique mirror, a perfect match to the table and chair, was my grandmother's. In fact, all of the furniture in this room was passed down to me from her. My grandfather moved it into my room when I was a little girl, once I had outgrown my crib, and I've had it ever since. The silver brush set, more for decoration than use, sits on the dresser. Next to it is a picture of the young woman it once belonged to. She definitely couldn't be described as pretty; her features were much too strong for that. But I've always taken comfort in her look of steadiness, her unwavering sense of self.

The Professor doesn't speak of my grandmother much, he never has. The things I've been able to glean about her over the years are from things I've read in his journals, though they were usually in reference to some historical debate or theory one of them was working on. Still, I have her straight nose.

She was a librarian at Oxford, and when I was young I used to go and sit in Bodley and imagine her filling the shelves with books. I first took the oath when I was eight; having read it once as a child I didn't need the prompts when it came the time.

I hereby undertake not to remove from the Library, nor to mark, deface, or injure in any way, any volume, document or other object belonging to it or in its custody; not to bring into the Library, or kindle therein, any fire or flame, and not to smoke in the Library; and I promise to obey all rules of the Library.

It all seemed so civilized to me. It still does really.

Putting my hands to my cheeks I pull my skin away from my eyes, trying to spread out the tired lines that never seem to disappear. My eyes travel upwards, to the hair that just won't seem to wave in the direction I want: the minute one side sits nicely the other decides it's time to act up and stick out in the opposite direction.

The vibration on my face causes me to look at my shaking hands, and I lower them. Panicking won't help anything. I have to be calm. If the police or reporters come around–

The thought alone causes me to almost lose my dinner. Breathing deeply through my nose, I let the long breaths out through my mouth. Over and over again I repeat this until the panic subsides to mere nausea.

It didn't go well, tonight. I think that much is quite clear, and I am under no sort of disillusionment that my chance to join the Alliance is firmly in the bin.

But I feel I have far bigger things to worry about at the

present time– namely if that really was the Shield of Quell and how exactly it got into the Ashmolean to begin with. If the Shield was stolen… if they can't find out who did it… they will come after us. I know it. I need to figure out exactly where that Shield came from– and if it is even real– before it's too late.

Charles is a fool not to ask more questions about the acquirement. Or perhaps he did ask and just isn't telling me. Surely someone can't just pop a priceless artefact in the post box and walk away. It must have been delivered somehow; it must be able to be traced back to the benefactor.

Who are they and how did they come to originally acquire the Shield? Was my grandfather confused all those years ago? The questions seem endless. I sit and contemplate what I should do next.

First things first, I need to make sure that Charles found the Shield. I try not to laugh at the sheer ridiculousness of the fact that he lost it about five minutes after he was put in charge of it. And the Alliance! What will they think when the people who were recruited to guard the piece managed to lose it right out from under their own noses? I wouldn't be surprised if they were all disbanded from the secret society immediately.

I know Charles said he was going to try and keep my name out of it, but I really don't see how that is possible. The Alliance knows who I am even if no one else does. They will know I was there. He will have to explain my absence to them, surely, and I realise that Charles may have finally found a problem he can't simply just talk his way out of.

When I first met Charles in university I could tell he was a charmer. That much was clear after all of five minutes. He'd already made his way through most of the women in our Ancient Artefacts class– albeit the number of females was small in comparison to the men who seemed to fill every chair.

I asked a question on the preservation of canvasses during the lecture and I could feel Charles watching me. I knew he was beginning to take an interest in me, but the feeling wasn't mutual. He was handsome and all, but I was focused on my studies. I was focused on making my grandfather proud and I knew history, more than a rich boyfriend, was the way to succeed at that.

After class he approached me to strike up a conversation but I couldn't stay, saying I had to get home. I had rented a small flat at school to give myself a bit of freedom. I was only there for a few months before the Professor's condition began to deteriorate and I came back home, driving to school every day instead.

"Let me walk you then," Charles offered, taking the books out of my hands before I even had a chance to reply.

"Thank you, but I'm quite capable of walking myself," I argued, taking my books back.

"Independence, I like that," Charles nodded, jogging to keep up with my quick strides. "You're June, right?"

"Right," I said, nodding in confirmation. "And you're the biggest flirt in class."

He stopped walking, putting his hand to his heart as though I wounded him before quickly running to catch up with me.

"Honesty: I like that too," he said, taking my books from my hands again before I could stop him. "Do you like Ancient Artefacts, June?"

"You know I do; I'm one of the only girls in the class. Why would I take it if I wasn't interested in it?" I asked him, trying to pick up my pace so I could get home and get rid of him.

"Less girls to compete for the men's attention?" Charles quipped to which I only rolled my eyes. "You can't tell me you don't fancy any of the blokes in there, there are tons to choose from."

"The only thing I fancy is history," I said, even though I knew it sounded ridiculous.

"Wow, a challenge. I think I like that best of all," he said, offering me a grin.

"Don't you have somewhere else you could be?" I asked him. I crossed the street, slipping through the gap of cars that stopped at the light.

"Not really," he said, shrugging his shoulders. "My parents are rich, so I don't have to have a job. My teachers are my parent's friends, so I don't really have to study."

"Must be nice," I said, though really I thought it sounded

awful.

"It's okay," he answered, non-committedly. "So you see, I have all the time in the world to chase you."

"Well, you're wasting your breath, because unlike you, I'm *not* rich and I *do* have to study," I said, reaching the small townhouse which housed my flat.

"No you don't, your grandfather is the Professor. It's not like he is going to fail you," Charles argued.

I frowned at him, "How did you know he was my grandfather?"

"You have the same last name," he pointed out. "And my parents told me."

"You discussed me with your parents?" I raised my eyebrow.

"They just mentioned you because they were talking about your grandfather–" Charles noticed his slip of the tongue and quickly smiled. "We were just talking."

"You mean your parents were debating whether my grandfather is a thief or not," I said, taking back my books from his hands. "You can tell them from the horse's mouth that he isn't."

I turned to walk inside but Charles touched my arm to stop me, and something inside of me decided to turn and look at his face.

"I don't need to; that's exactly what I said to them last night." He offered me another smile before dropping his hand.

I didn't say anything else, just walked into my flat and watched him walk back towards the university from the front window.

The following day I went to class and the seat next to him was empty. I put my knapsack down beside him and sat down behind the empty desk.

"Thank you," I said, not looking at him.

"You don't need to thank people for saying the truth June," Charles replied, obviously knowing what I was referring to. "It's when they tell a big fat lie for you that you owe them a favour."

I turned to look at his smiling face, which managed to coax one onto my own lips.

"Do you always wear those glasses?" he asked, pointing to my black-rimmed spectacles that were another hand me down from my grandmother.

"Yes," I said.

"They suit you."

"What are you even doing here?" I asked, noticing he didn't bring a notepad or pencil with him to class. "Do you even like Ancient Artefacts?"

"No," he admitted, not looking caught out in the slightest by the admission. "But it's the furthest thing away from what my father wanted me to do so I decided to major in it."

That produced a real smile on my face.

"What does he want you to be?"

"Banker," he said. "I've never met a happy banker, have you?"

I shrugged my shoulders because I didn't really know any adults that weren't somehow connected to the world of archaeology or art history.

"Tell you what, you try not to get in my pants every five minutes and I will help you pass this class," I said, pointing to the Professor who was standing at the front waiting to get started. "Because he won't pass you without merit no matter who your parents are."

Charles nodded and took my outstretched hand. "It's a deal."

At the end of the lecture, Charles picked up my notebook before I even had a chance.

"I noticed you don't have a textbook," he said, looking down at my notebook filled with handwriting. "Is it because you're already guaranteed an A?"

"Hardly," I shook my head, fully aware that the Professor took history far too seriously to pass someone who didn't deserve it. "I don't need the textbook, I've memorized it."

Charles laughed, obviously thinking I was joking.

"I have," I argued. "I have an eidetic memory."

"Right," Charles nodded and then frowned. "What's that?"

"It means basically anything I see or read I remember for a very long time, some things forever."

"So you read the whole textbook and now you've memorized it?" he asked, and I could hear the note of disbelief in his voice.

"The whole thing," I answered.

"Bullshit," he said, shaking his head.

"It's true. I've had it since I was a child, usually you grow out of it but I am the one in a million that managed to hang onto it."

"So I could show you anything and you would remember?" he asked, looking around the hallway. "Look at that poster."

I turned my head to look over my shoulder, and studied the picture for ten seconds before turning back around. "Go."

"What colour is her hair?" he asked.

"Seriously?" I rolled my eyes. "Blond, and anyone would remember that. Ask me something really detailed."

He squinted at the poster before looking at me again. "What is the second last word in the subtitle?"

"Buy," I said firmly.

"What colour is her nail polish?"

"Pink," I answered.

"How many flowers are on her jumper?"

I closed my eyes, counting in my head. "Eighteen."

I opened my eyes to see Charles also counting the flowers. "That's weird."

I smiled.

"So why do you even bother going to class then, if you already know everything?" he asked as we resumed walking down the hallway.

"Because textbooks just give you the facts, I want to learn what's *not* in the textbooks."

Charles studied me before shaking his head. "You keep getting weirder."

Chapter Eight

I make us both a cup of tea and get the Professor dressed in his pyjamas and slippers. He gets settled in front of the television in the sitting room, his notebook in his hand, waiting for the evening news to start. Lately, he's taken to writing down anything he finds interesting on the news to investigate on his own. "Can't trust a bloody word out of their mouths, June Bug," he argues.

I've changed into my corduroy brown skirt and my comfy wool sweater, pulling the sides of my hair back into two clips. I know I will have to put my pyjamas on in an hour or so, but I wore this outfit on my first day of teaching and it's always seemed to bring me a bit of luck. I'm hoping it won't fail me now. Peeking my head through the doorway, I see the Professor fully engrossed in the evening news, the journals and newspaper clippings left strewn on the side of the chair, untouched from earlier. That's relieving, I was sure after what just happened he would be combing through the articles again. But that's the interesting thing with his disease, when your life is in trouble, you sometimes welcome the brief respite of not remembering. Most days there are only small blocks of time where he doesn't remember; forgetting simple things like where he put things, or what he was planning to do. Then there are days like today where he wanders in a daze, more moments of delirium than reality. I worry more and more about the future, and that soon these bad days will not be the exception, but the rule.

They were able to catch it early, mainly because of his forgetful moments at work. Dr Cooke, his colleague at the university, was the first to bring it to everyone's attention. The doctors started him on medication, and it had worked initially; for weeks he went without an incident. After I finished my degree I became his assistant, earning my own doctorate at the time, and I was able to cover things. Prompt him during lectures if he lost his place, even take over the lesson if necessary. Then, over the past few years or so it began to slowly worsen. He was asked to retire two years ago. I thought removing the strain of teaching would be good for him, but all it did was give him more time to obsess: obsess over the accusations, he spends most of his days in his study, combing through his old journals. On the bad days he gets manic with the articles, clipping them out and creating new journals. Conspiracy journals.

While I'm at work I have help come in; home caregivers fix him lunch and tidy the house. But in the past six months his health has declined. He'd have a bad day and I would get the call at work: "It might be time to think about alternative arrangements. We just aren't equipped to look after someone with such demanding needs."

But I couldn't do that to the Professor. A nursing home would kill him, I know it. He was such a remarkable man. He still is, I remind myself. If it weren't for the bloody Shield!

Perhaps Charles was right, and this is the answer that we have both been looking for. Now that the Shield has been found it lifts the scandal off of the Professor. I know he didn't discover it twenty years ago. The Professor's whole life has been dedicated to the study and preservation of history; he would have never found that Shield and then kept it for his own personal gain. He would have wanted the world to see it; it would have been his finest hour.

Feeling confident that the Professor is settled for the time being, I walk down the hall and enter his study. The walls are lined with dark walnut bookcases, all housing books the Professor has read repeatedly over the years. He used to love to read the classics, collecting first editions. Now all he focuses on reading are those articles about the Shield.

Stepping around the big desk in the centre of the room, I pull back the chair and sit down. The left hand drawer is meant to hold file folders, but when I pull it open it is crammed with all of his journals. He used to fill them out nightly: his thoughts and experiences of the day.

I can tell the top few are all from recent years, filled with his clippings, the pages wrinkled from the glue. I pick them up, and set them on top of the desk so I'm able to see more journals underneath, which look like the ones that I will need. The earthy brown leather, worn over the years, makes me smile. I used to buy him a journal every year for Christmas, and every year leading up to it he used to laugh, "Getting low on pages now June Bug, I'll have to start writing on the walls soon…" Then when he unwrapped his gift at Christmas he would shoot me a sly smile. "How did you know?"

I pick up the journal now at the top and start to flip through it. It's dated 1961, the year the Professor joined the volunteer efforts at Fishbourne for the Roman Residence. A man fixing a sewer line had come across the outside boundaries for a building, which later turned out to be a Roman Palace. It was one of the first excavations the Professor had been a part of as a young man. Tucked neatly inside the journal is a picture of a young Professor, standing by the dig site, shovels and other tools scattered at his feet. The breeze blows his hair; his white shirt soiled with the ground's dirt. Dark suspenders hold up his light pants. A wide smile is on his face; the excitement of what he was a part of evident in his eyes. One arm on his hip, the other wrapped around the shoulder of another man who looks just as thrilled. Flipping the picture over I see the Professor's writing on the back. *Daniel and I, Fishbourne, 1961.*

Not dwelling on the picture any longer, I tuck it back in the journal and place it with the others on the desk.

Roughly a dozen journals later and I finally manage to find the one I'm searching for.

1991 is written on the first page in the left-hand corner. I flip through to the middle. The excavation started earlier in the year, but it took months to get to the tomb.

I have read this all before, more times than I care to remember. The Professor would bring them out so often in recent years, making me read them over and over again.

The Sutton-Hoo excavation team was quite vast; the Professor and Dr Cooke just part of one of the many teams sent to study the different mounds, not to mention the dozens of volunteers that were eager to get their chance to be a part of such an important discovery. Several mounds were uncovered and studied, though so many still remain untouched for future archaeologists.

His notes are extensive, detailing the different techniques that were used to remove the soil, techniques that were new to the field at the time. Previously, most of the excavation process was done by hand, but during the late seventies machines were becoming very popular to do the grunt work. With new equipment they were able to do an ultrasound of the earth below to see how deep the soil went. Towards the latter half of the journal his writing begins to get more anxious.

September 14, 1991

We are so very close now, and the anticipation is palpable. Daniel tells me not to get my hopes up. Most of the other tombs that have already been uncovered are empty, robbed of their riches. Each time my heart sinks, the thought of those precious artefacts gone— perhaps lost forever. But there are other things we are able to glean from the sites even when they seem empty. For instance, an interesting ritual seems to have taken place for the young nobleman buried in the mound we uncovered last month based on the way his limbs were laid. The young pups here talk of the gold and the silver, how incomprehensible it is that all of this has been kept underground, walked over for centuries on the family's estate. They spend their nights speculating about what they would do if they were able to stumble across something on their own land, many promising to start digging holes when they return home. A young volunteer is convinced his Grandfather has an old dagger in his attic that once belonged to an ancient warrior, which makes the others' eyes light up with interest. I'm sure they will be paying their own relatives a visit over the holidays to have a root through their cupboards. Even some older volunteers seem to be swept up in the excitement. A man of my age has joined the excavation efforts this week, and he seems terribly eager to learn all there is to know about my vast knowledge on the Anglo-Saxons, constantly asking me to appease his curious mind with speculations as to what we might find. I must confess my ego is beginning to enjoy our nightly conversations. For those of us who have been in it long enough, we know that there are riches that far exceed the value of their gold. The insight we can gain from the detailed carvings, how they can be the confirmation of an entire tribe that were doubted to even exist! The illustrations a means of keeping history alive for those who were illiterate to pass down to their kingdoms. Daniel and I let them have their dreams, though. One day they will learn the meaning of priceless.

A smile touches my lips; my fingers gently touch the page

of the man who gave his life to the past.

Flipping over the next few pages, I find the entry I am looking for.

September 20th, 1991

It happened. We opened the tomb today, the split oak in marvellous condition considering its age, showing most of its wear at the binding around the outside. The morning didn't start off well, lost the bloody crowbars if you can believe it. I must have put them down next to the toilets and forgotten about them. We lost some daylight searching, but luckily the top came away surprisingly easily, far more than the other tombs they uncovered last week.

The sun was so bright, flooding the hollow ground with natural light, we couldn't have asked for better conditions. When the top was removed I actually reached for Daniel's hand. I'm sure he will remind me of that in the days to come over a pint. A light came from inside the tomb, blinding my eye for a moment. Daniel was called away though, there had been a collapse at another mound and our team was needed. Someone had to stay with the tomb; we couldn't leave it unguarded like that so soon after opening it in case the ground suddenly settled from the disturbance. I know I should have waited, but the impatience stirring inside of me wouldn't settle. I had to see what was inside, so I climbed down the ladder. Stupid, I know. Terribly dangerous, Daniel reminded me when he returned. But it was all for naught. The tomb, like so many of the others before it, was empty. I was just about to climb back up, pretend to the others I hadn't been down, when I saw it. We are lucky our ladder's poles had not disturbed it. I must have stepped right past it in my hurry to get down, my footprint missing the outer imprint by inches. My impatience nearly disturbing history, something that I have warned the volunteers about for years. Dreadfully embarrassing really.

But it remains intact: the unmistakable markings of something that had been buried with the young man in the grave. The detail quite remarkable considering its age and how the ground must have settled over the centuries. An offering, no doubt, to honour the nobleman. I'm not sure what it could have been; it too probably taken by grave robbers. Daniel and I are eager to return tomorrow to study the markings some more, though I am sad to say the discovery—or lack of discovery as some see it— has discouraged some of the volunteers, and caused some of them to pack it in early. My eager pupil has even abandoned the cause when he heard of a promising new dig in Sheffield. It may not be the treasure itself, but the markings alone could prove to be of great historical significance.

I close my eyes and think about all the circumstances of that day. What would his life have been like if that other mound hadn't collapsed? If only he hadn't been so impatient! If only he had waited until the others returned!

October 1st, 1991

The commissioners have sent our team home, and right at the pinnacle of the discovery. There are still many mounds left that are set to be uncovered, and yet they send us home? It's preposterous. Something about the funding beginning to dwindle. I would have stayed for nothing if they had allowed it! The markings have been photographed and I take some solace in the fact that they have allowed Daniel and I to continue to study them as they've shipped them back to Oxford. Still,

June isn't set to return from school for another few weeks for the holidays, and I do wish they had let us stay on for just a little longer. On top of it all, I can't seem to find my glasses anywhere, which is giving me a dreadful headache.

I flip through the journal, seeing notes of his about the markings and the research he and Dr Cooke continued working on when they arrived home. My eye catches another entry, and the feverish writing makes me stop and read it.

December 1st, 1991

Something is wrong. I'm not sleeping well. An image keeps flashing in my mind, popping in at various times. In the middle of a lecture, I'll be explaining the use of burhs and I'll forget what I was about to say, instead the image remains the only thing I can think about. I think it has something to do with Sutton-Hoo. My mind is imagining things that it could not possibly be recalling. Why? Why is the image so clear? My hands are holding it in my dreams, and although I do not know where I am I feel a sense of panic. Daniel tells me to put it out of my mind. June seemed concerned when she visited on the weekend. She worries I'm not eating enough, bless her.

I fight back the tears that rim my eyes. Closing the journal, I put it down on the desk, my hands resting on it. At the top of the back cover I feel something sticking out and pick it back up. Opening to the back cover I see the Professor has stuffed a folded piece of paper in the back pocket of the journal. It is probably just a page that has fallen out over the years, but I take it out anyways for curiosity sake.

I gasp, my hand flying to my mouth to choke back the

sob when I look at the drawing on the piece of paper. It is an exact likeness of the Shield that I saw at the museum just hours ago. The boss so intricately drawn by the Professor's steady hand. The groupings of the gems in grape-like clusters, almost identical to the rubies and garnets on the Shield itself. The leatherwork that covered the piece seems to be in better care in his drawing, it reaching to the full edges of the wood, but other than this small detail it is an exact likeness.

My hands begin to shake uncontrollably. He's never once shown me this. Why has he never shown me this? Twenty years of rants, of articles strewn over the house, of reading his journals to me over and over again. Why would he keep this hidden from me? All this time, did he secretly doubt himself?

The Shield was preserved so well. I thought at the Ashmolean that the person who had it all this time must have known how to take care of it. Oh God, why does he have this drawing?

Pushing the chair back, I grab the journal with my other hand, and walk out of the study.

I find the Professor in the exact same position I left him in, dipping his biscuits into his tea.

"Professor," I say, kneeling in front of him. "I need to ask you about this."

I place the drawing in his lap, my hand still shaking.

Frowning, he looks down, but when his eyes fix on the

drawing he blinks rapidly.

"Bogwash," he shakes his head, looking back up at the screen.

"Did you draw this?" I ask, pointing to the paper again.

His eyes actively avoid the drawing as his teacup begins to rattle on its saucer.

"Professor, please," I plead with him, putting my hand on his forearm. "I'm going to help you, I'm going to fix this. But, I need to know what this is."

His eyes lock onto me, shimmering with tears.

"It wasn't there, June. I swear it," he whispers to me, before lowering his hand so that it covers the drawing.

I nod, unsure what to do next.

My phone rings and I launch to my feet. Running over to the sideboard where I left my purse, I fish inside of it for my phone.

I press the button for the screen to light up and find there is a message waiting for me.

June, it's Max. They are coming for you. Get out of your house.

Startled at the message, my fingers fly over the keys.

Who is coming? What is going on? Have you found the Shield?

I click send, my whole body vibrating in panic. I look over at the Professor, who is still sitting in his chair, his eyes staring at his hand over the single piece of paper.

My phone rings again.

There is no time. The Shield is still missing. I'm not supposed to be telling you this. Get out of your house. I will contact you when I can.

How can this be happening? I look at the phone in my hand, reading the words over and over again, before it rings again.

Now, June!

I look down and see my leather knapsack sitting beside the table, full of the papers I brought home for the weekend to read. I lean down, unzip the bag, and dump the papers on the floor. Grabbing my purse and phone, I shove them in the bag and quickly run to the front door to retrieve my boots and coat, throwing the Professor's loafers in the knapsack as well.

Running back to the sitting room, I reach the Professor and grab his hand.

"Professor, we have to leave, now," I say urgently, trying to pull him up from his chair.

"I haven't finished the news yet," he says, peering around me.

"Nothing happened today," I reach for the remote and turn off the barely visible screen.

"It's a bit late to go out, June," the Professor moans, putting his teacup down on the table beside him. "I was thinking of going to bed, actually."

"No, Professor, we have to leave," I look up when I see what looks like car headlights pass through the window at the side of the house. Someone is driving down the side lane. Someone is *coming.* I've got to get the Professor out. I have to get that drawing out of this house.

"I've had a long day," he pouts, moving his hand to cup the side of his face.

"Professor, please!" I beg, trying to pull his arm, to make him stand up.

It could be those reporters. I should have known they would come here as soon as they heard the Shield had resurfaced.

"Honestly, June, what could be so bloody important?" he says, reluctantly standing up, but not moving any further than that.

"I—" I hear the sound of car doors outside, as I add the journal and his drawing into the backpack. "I want to go and buy whiskey!"

"Oh," he says and suddenly all of the weariness he displayed before is gone. "You should have mentioned that earlier. Always time left in the day for a good drink."

I put the backpack on and take the Professor's arm, leading him into the kitchen.

"Why are we going out the back door?" he asks, picking up a biscuit that was left on the counter from earlier and taking a bite.

"It's a shortcut," I explain. I whip the back door open and wince as the glass panes rattle on the window set into the wood. I hear someone pounding on the front door, so I shove the Professor outside and carefully close the door behind me, trying not to make a sound.

"Is that the hired car?" the Professor asks, looking over his shoulder as I lead him into the yard.

"No, probably a salesman," I answer. Once outside I can hear voices at the front, and realize it's only a matter of time until they force their way in or try to go around the back.

"Quickly, Professor!" I whisper and guide him across the large yard to the weeping willow. I stop walking when we reach the thick hedges that line our property with the back road.

A sharp sound runs through the air and I turn back to the house, realizing that they probably used something to get through the front door. I take a step backwards, but an icy chill runs over my body as someone puts their hand over my mouth.

Chapter Nine

"June, it's me!" I hear the voice in my ear but I have to turn and look Griffin in the eye before I can let myself believe it's him. He puts a finger to his lips.

"Ah good!" the Professor says, clapping Griffin on the back. "Just about to nip to the shops for whiskey."

The Professor strolls past Griffin, ducking down through the hedges that line our property and shield it from the neighbouring estates.

"What are you doing here?" I hiss, looking over my shoulder as the torchlights shine through the lower level of our house.

"Come with me." He grabs my arm, propelling me forward.

I trip over my own feet, but manage to right myself. I stumble through the hedges behind the Professor.

Griffin's black car is idling on the other side of the hedge. The Professor has already made himself comfortable in the back seat.

"Get in!" Griffin orders, opening my door and running around to his own. He constantly checks over his shoulder for anyone who may be watching.

"I– what are you doing here?" I repeat, but I hear some voices not too far away on the other side of the hedge, so I slide in the car and buckle my seatbelt.

"Hold on," Griffin puts the car into gear and quickly peels out onto the road.

"Who are those people?" I demand, looking over my shoulder at the hedges surrounding our property and watch them as they grow smaller and smaller. "If those are reporters, they are trespassing! They can't enter our house without our consent. We should be calling the police!"

"You can't do that," Griffin argues. "Either they *are* the police, or whoever is in your home would be long gone by the time the coppers ever showed up and you'd sound like a raving lunatic."

"This is crazy," I say, putting my knapsack on top of my knees. I open the zipper to check my mobile, but I haven't received any messages. "I need to go to a police station."

"And say what? You don't seem to even know what's happening right now," Griffin says. "No, we need to get as far away from here as possible. Going to your own home was a bad idea."

"What are you talking about? What do you know about all this?"

"Me? I know nothing, besides the fact that you may or may not have stolen a shield, and now someone wants it back," he says, speeding through an amber light while checking his rear-view mirror. "I saw those idiots pull up in front of your house looking highly suspicious. Don't they know you never park outside of the person's actual house?"

He snorts, shaking his head in amusement.

"Highly suspicious?" I ask, watching as his eyes dart down the different streets as we pass them. "Who are you, Columbo?"

"Well, they didn't look like they were there to sell you Avon," he retorts. "I figured they must be at your place to look for the shield you stole, or they've come to take the Professor away."

"First off, I didn't steal anything," I turn to face him, my face growing red. "And second, why were you lurking around my house?"

"You're missing the point," Griffin brushes off my question. "Whether you have the Shield or not doesn't matter; what matters is they *think* you have it."

"Well, I don't have it!" I repeat. Thinking about it now I realise I acted too impulsively at the house. Max's messages scared me, but thinking it through now, running doesn't seem like something an innocent person would do. The reporter's will only speculate more about our absence.

"We need to go back and tell them that I don't have it. Let them search! I have nothing to hide," I cross my arms defensively over my chest.

It might be a good idea to rip up the Professor's drawing, though.

"You said we were going for whiskey." The Professor

pouts from the backseat. "I'm not getting out of this bloody car again unless a bottle of Jack's finest is in my hand!"

"You think they are going to give up that easily?" Griffin ridicules.

"I'm going to get them to listen to reason," I calmly argue.

"Let's say– for argument's sake– you *don't* have the Shield and they can't find it in your house. Do you think they are just going to shrug their shoulders and say 'Oh well'? They'll think you've hidden it somewhere!" Griffin speaks to me in a tone that suggest he is trying to explain something simple to a five year old.

"Charles would never let anyone hurt me, he knows I don't have it. I'll just call him–" I pick up my phone.

"Is this the same man who told you to leave the scene of a crime at the Ashmolean? The same man who told you to lay low by going to your *own home*?" He snorts.

"What are you suggesting?" I ask him. "Charles is my friend!"

"And he's the one who warned you to get out of there?" Griffin asks, navigating the car around the corner.

My silence is my answer.

"Or maybe he's the one that *sent* those people to your house in the first place. I mean, he is the one that ordered you to leave the museum, who told you to go to the exact place they went looking for you," he suggests, and the doubt is enough to make me lower my phone.

This is crazy; the whole thing is insane. Charles is my *friend*, and although it may seem crazy, considering what has just happened, I trust him. I've known him for over ten years. He's always protected me. He helped me find care for the Professor over the last few years as things became increasingly difficult. He wouldn't send those people after me. If anything, he must have gotten word that someone was coming for me and told Max to warn me. There must be some reason he couldn't warn me himself.

"So, what do you suggest I do?" I ask Griffin.

"We lie low," he says, as though the answer is obvious. "Just like your so-called *friend* told us to do until we figure this out."

"What *we*? You keep saying *we,* but there is no *we!*" I throw my hands up in the air. "There's just me and the Professor who are up shit's creek without a paddle!"

"Language, June," the Professor admonishes from the backseat, pointing to Griffin. "We have company."

"Well, there was a *we* when you needed my help getting away from the museum," Griffin comments.

"That was different," I argue. "I don't even understand what you are doing here. Why were you at my house?"

"Listen, I've been thinking about what you said earlier, about not wanting to ruin my illustrious career by smearing my good name with a scandalous trial of greed and intrigue."

"I don't believe I phrased it quite like that…"

"Either way," Griffin shrugs, merging onto the

roundabout, "I've decided to take the risk."

I look at him dumbfounded.

"Oh, you have?" I say, making my tone as sarcastic as possible. "How honourable of you!"

"Listen, you say you are innocent, and I believe you," he shrugs. "But, if it turns out you are a thieving liar we'll just say I knew nothing about it and was only paid to drive you around."

He taps the dashboard where he's turned the taxi's meter on.

"This is too much," I say, shaking my head and looking around at the carnage of my normal, civilized life.

"You need my help, June," Griffin lowers his voice. "You can't figure this out *and* look after the Professor at the same time."

"And you want to help me out of the goodness of your heart?" I sceptically stare at his profile.

"I help you now, you help me when this is over," he says, turning the car onto the motorway.

"What does that mean?"

"I'll be honest with you—"

"There's a novel idea," I interrupt.

He continues as though I didn't speak. "My plays aren't doing very well. I mean— the writing is top notch," he amends, "but unless you're bloody Harold Pinter, they don't give a toss if you've got talent or not."

"Must be hard," I say, and try to tamper down my anger

at the complete narcissism of the man sitting beside of me.

"But the public you see, they love a good hero. Or a good scandal, either would work for me," he shrugs his shoulders. "I reckon a few days with you, and Ian McKellen will be knocking on my door, begging to be in one of my plays. You know what they say: any publicity is good publicity."

"You've got to be kidding—"

"Now, June Bug," the Professor leans forward to settle his hand on the headrest of my seat. "The young chap here has made some fine logical arguments, his formulas are actually quite sound, albeit he could use a little work on the delivery."

I peer over my shoulder to see the Professor's blue eyes.

"Never say no to an ally, that's my motto," the Professor smiles before lowering his voice. "Also, we don't currently own a vehicle, so stop berating the young man or else we'll never get to the bloody shops."

He pats me on the shoulder before leaning back in his seat, joyfully looking out the window again.

I have to admit, begrudgingly mind you, that what the Professor said actually makes sense. We sold the car a few months ago because I couldn't trust the Professor to drive anymore. I tried taking his keys away at first, but I would wake up in the middle of the night to the sound of him driving our car into the neighbour's carport. I decided hired cars and public transport would be the best course for the future.

The Professor's little speech also makes me realise something else. I have to start thinking about this logically. If I don't have the Shield, then someone else does.

"Fine," I say through gritted teeth. "But it won't be a few days. I just need to go to one address and this should all be cleared up."

"That soon?" Griffin argues, but after glimpsing my death stare he adds, "No, er– great. The sooner the better, I say. So what is this one address?"

"I want to see an old friend," I answer him, writing down the address in one of the Professor's notebooks and showing it to Griffin, not wanting to say the familiar address out loud in front of the Professor.

"Great," he nods. "And they will be able to help us because…"

"Because they are the only other person who knows anything about the Shield," I say as quietly as possible. I peek over my shoulder to see if the Professor is listening, but I see that he has nodded off again. Honestly, that man can fall asleep at the drop of a hat.

"Were they at the museum?" he asks, slowing the car down. "I thought we agreed it wasn't a good idea to contact anyone who was at the museum."

"First of all, there is no *we* here. There is no *us*. So if you could stop saying that I think I would have a better chance of not wanting to throttle you every five seconds," I say, clutching my knapsack. "And secondly, he wasn't at the museum."

"Okay," Griffin lifts his hands off the steering wheel, briefly, in a defensive gesture. "So if he wasn't at the museum, how is he going to be able to help us– er– you?"

"Because he is the one who accused the Professor of stealing it," I whisper.

"Wasn't that your friend Charles?" he asks.

"No, Charles accused him today. Or me... He accused one of us today," I say, getting confused with my own thoughts. "Dr Cooke accused the Professor twenty years ago of stealing the Shield."

"Wow, this Shield sounds like the old boyfriend who just won't take no for an answer," Griffin tries to joke, but my icy glare makes him look straight ahead again.

"So, what are we hoping to get out of this Dr Cooke?" Griffin asks.

"Answers."

"I feel I am missing something here," he purses his lips.

I close my eyes slowly. If I thought it was at all a possibility that we could make the rest of the drive to the Cotswolds in silence, I wouldn't answer. As it is though, I know Griffin will keep pestering me with questions, and between his questions and the puzzling thoughts that are streaming through my head, I am starting to get an awful headache.

"Dr Cooke and the Professor used to be partners. They

were funded under the same program at Oxford for their archaeological digs. They were–" the word catches in my throat. "They were best mates."

I look at Griffin, who clearly thinks this explains nothing.

"How much do you know about the Anglo-Saxon burial mounds at Sutton-Hoo?" I ask him.

He glances at me from the corner of his eye before quickly returning his attention to the road. "Oh, you know, this and that…"

I roll my eyes.

"The mounds at Sutton-Hoo contained what we now have as the greatest collection of metalwork and art history from the Middle Ages, roughly the fifth to the eleventh century."

"And the Anglo-Saxons, they were… umm… important?"

"I thought you said you went to university! Did they not teach you anything at Leeds?" I ask, flabbergasted.

"It was years ago!" he says defensively. "How am I supposed to remember all of that?"

I shoot him a disapproving look before continuing. "At the collapse of the Roman Empire, several centuries of Germanic tribes emigrated to the southern half of the island from continental Europe."

"Wait– so, technically we're German, not English?" he asks, puzzled.

"*Germanic*, not *German*," I say, and have to calm my temper. "It means that they came from all over, and adopted the new culture."

"Oh, of course." Griffin nods.

I breathe in deeply. "Several centuries of *Germanic*," I pause for emphasis, "immigration resulted in Kingdoms being developed. Many of the Anglo-Saxon innovations are still in place today, including our regional government, the re-establishment of Christianity, languages, and literature such as Beowulf…"

Griffin seems a little more interested in the subject.

"Never could get through that one," he says. "The old English always muddles me up. Don't have a clue what they're on about."

"Old English that comes from the Anglo-Saxons," I say, excited that he is at least listening to me. "Our charters and laws derive from them as well."

"Okay, I get it. They started some good stuff."

I tell myself not to scream.

"So, they also invented the Shield or something?" he asks.

"No, they didn't invent the Shield!" Honestly, God must be testing me. "The Shield of Quell is rumoured to be a gift given by arguably the greatest King in Anglo-Saxon history, King Raedwald, to his son before fighting in a war that changed the course of history as we know it."

I end there on a breathless note. I really do enjoy talking

about the Anglo-Saxons, but I've always stayed away from it in my career, choosing the Renaissance as my field of specialty. Obviously, given the current circumstances, I believe that was a wise decision.

"Okay, I think I've got it," Griffin says. "This King Raedwald might have given his son a shield, which might have been buried in one of the mounds at Sutton-Hoo, which might have been discovered by your grandfather, who might have nicked it."

"Forgetting all of the circumstantial parts to that equation, yes," I say, nodding.

"Right," Griffin says, brushing his hair out of his eyes. "And now we are going to see the git who accused the Professor of nicking it in the first place?"

"Yes."

"And what happens when we get there?" he asks.

"Well," I say, weighing up my options. "I either find out what Dr Cooke and the Professor know and prove that the Shield never existed, thus rendering the one we are accused of stealing a fake. Or, I prove that it is the Shield of Quell, figure out who really stole it, and clear my grandfather's name."

We sit in silence for a moment, thinking about the two options.

"Seems simple enough," Griffin shrugs.

Chapter Ten

"I'll be fine!" I say to Griffin for what seems like the hundredth time. He shakes his head but we climb the front steps to Dr Cooke's house anyway.

The small cottage is half an hour from Oxford– close enough that the Professor and I used to visit frequently when I was a child. It looks much smaller than I remember. I wonder if my eidetic memory is conditional on the relativity of my size to the object I'm viewing. I'll have to research that when this is all sorted, it could be an interesting research paper.

The red brick on the outside is all but hidden by the moss that covers the front of the house, and the roof is in desperate need of repair. I suddenly have a memory of a lovely stone garden in the backyard where we used to take Sunday tea when I was a little girl.

"I don't like it," Griffin says, looking around. The neighbours are so few and far between that all that surrounds us is dark trees and meadows, so I'm not sure what he is on about. "What if someone followed us? This is somewhere they would *expect* you to go."

"I won't be long," I argue.

A loud noise echoes in the distance– it sounds like a dog's bark, and Griffin jumps, his back against my body in a protective gesture.

"This is a bad idea," he leans forward to look in the direction the sound came from. He finally steps away from me when the noise stops.

"Are you... are you *worried* about me?" I straighten my glasses on my nose as I watch his eyes dart around.

"What kind of question is that?" he stops his frantic twitching to look at me. "Of course I am!"

"I–" A blush rises to my cheeks; my hand instinctively reaches for my hair in a self-conscious gesture. I must look like a mess.

"What if someone finds you and bashes you on the head? Between you and the Professor, I won't have anyone who remembers what I'm doing here," he says, shaking his head before taking up his vigilant survey again.

I quickly lower my hand to my side.

"Stay out here and watch the Professor," I order before turning to knock on the front door.

I hear someone approach and then the lock is turned, the door yanked open.

"Hello–" Dr Cooke has a wide smile on his face when he first opens the door, but when he recognizes me he falters. "You're not the Chinese food."

"Afraid not, Dr Cooke."

We study each other. The years have been kind to him, but then again he always did have a youthful personality. He keeps his hair shorter than he used to, and I can see he's missing most from the top. His weight has taken an opposite approach to aging than the Professor's, his middle thicker than it once was, his face full. I guess that's what happens when you spend half your life making television and radio circuits, earning hundreds of thousands of pounds off of lies. That has to have bought him a cake or two.

"I– er– you've caught me at a bit of a bad time, I'm afraid, my dear," Dr Cooke says, and I can see the plan formulating across his features. "I'm expecting some company. Coming for tea, actually."

I look down at my watch. It's nearly midnight.

"But we really should catch up– I've been meaning to…" He doesn't seem to know which excuse will serve him better. "I'll give you a ring and set something up."

He offers me a smile, and starts to close the door.

"I'm afraid it can't wait, Dr Cooke," I block the door before he's able to close it. "It should only take a few minutes."

He stands in the doorway trying to think of his next excuse, but his eyes take in Griffin's stony face, and my hand that I haven't moved from the door. Finally he sighs and opens the door wide.

"If it's just a minute," he nods. "Though I can't imagine what could be this important."

He turns around and walks back into the cottage, leaving the door open for me to enter.

"Stay here and watch the Professor," I tell Griffin again, shooting him a warning glance.

I walk through the front door and turn around to close it before following Dr Cooke down the hall and into the sitting room on the left.

Once inside the room he takes a seat on the blue paisley covered settee. The fabric has clearly faded over the years, the blue all but impossible to see on the arms. Looking around the room I notice not much else is in better care. I can see where there had been paintings on the walls at one point, the wallpaper darker where the rectangular shaped frames used to hang. The carpet is threadbare and ripped under the small table that sits in the middle of the room. Clasping his hands together in his lap, Dr Cooke sits and watches me survey the room.

"I think you know why I am here," I say, taking a seat on the green plaid wingback chair by the door.

"I have no idea," he says, briefly raising his hand to scratch his head.

"I'm here about the Shield of Quell."

Although he must know this is the reason for my visit I notice the nervous twitch in his eye that starts as soon as I mention the Shield.

"What about it?" he asks, studying the threadbare carpet under his feet.

"Well, let's start with the question as to why you would accuse my grandfather of stealing it twenty years ago."

"Now, wait a minute! I did no such thing. All I said was I had seen something, a glint of something, reflecting off the sun. Your grandfather went in before me, even though he knew we were meant to go in together. I was back not ten minutes later, and by the time I climbed down I could see there was nothing in there, just some outer markings of a circular piece on the ground."

"Oh really? And that's what filled the pages of your bestselling book, was it?" I ask, and he at least has the decency to look embarrassed.

"Bestselling book," he snorts, lifting his eyes to the ceiling. "It hasn't stopped the roof from caving in, has it? Bloody royalties aren't worth shit."

"I'm surprised, people usually love a tale of lies and betrayal."

"I loved your grandfather," he says, as though it's the only defence he needs. "You two were like family to me."

"And that's how you treat your family?" I argue. "At the first chance of stardom you throw them to the wolves?"

"I didn't throw anyone to the wolves!" he raises his voice. "No one thought a single word of it– of us not finding anything in that mound. The other archaeologists were convinced that there was never anything down there– a trick of the eye in the sun's light. Your grandfather was the one that put doubt in everyone's mind!"

"What are you talking about?"

"I'm talking about when we were back at Oxford. We had to meet with the commissioners of the dig to go over our findings, show them our notes. It's very typical procedure even if nothing was discovered besides dirt. But your grandfather couldn't leave well enough alone. He started going off on a rant about the Shield, how he had *seen* it. He tried to show us the drawings he had done in his journal, but I managed to grab it out of his hands. I tried to appease them, tell them he wasn't feeling well, but it raised so many eyebrows," Dr Cooke shakes his head, leaning back on the couch. "The commissioners kept digging, asking questions. I confronted your grandfather multiple times. There were times when he didn't have a clue what I was talking about, telling me I know as much as he did, that there was no shield in that tomb. Other times..."

Dr Cooke closes his eyes and exhales deeply.

"Other times he would come and find me while I was in a lecture, the journal in his hand, ranting about the lost Shield and claiming he'd seen it with his own eyes," he looks up at me. "They began to suspect *me*, June. To suspect that we were conspiring together, that we had somehow stolen the Shield. These people, the people who pay for these excavations, you want to believe they are investing in history, but really it all comes down to the dollars and cents. To possess something of that value... I tried to convince them he was unwell–"

"But when you couldn't you decided to save yourself," I don't even attempt to hide the disgust in my voice. "He isn't well!"

"I thought it would go away," he explains, "that they would begin to see what those closest to him had already begun to witness. He was starting to forget things, little things. Sometimes it would be weeks without a single incident. You have to understand... the commissioners' questions... their relentless interrogations... it went on for *years*. I *never* said that your grandfather stole the Shield."

The adamant denial in his voice causes me to shake my head.

"Yes, but you stopped saying he didn't steal it."

We study each other before he nods once, lowering his gaze.

I remember the day so vividly. Sometimes, because of my eidetic memory I find memories of the things I can't read or see, or how I felt in a certain situation or what someone said to me, are things I'm able to forget easily. They aren't as easy for me to hold onto. But the day when the newspapers broke the story of the Shield is a day that I can't ever forget. The Professor had a rather difficult lecture, stumbling through how museums preserve artefacts. I ended up taking over the class while the Professor sat in the corner, offering me a grateful smile whenever I would look in his direction. When I spoke to him afterwards he told me he had been contacted by the paper, and they told him Dr

Cooke had retracted his statement about the Professor's innocence.

That was the beginning of many bad days to come.

"You think it has been easy for me, do you? I've lost everything because of that Shield, because of an old man's ramblings! They made me take early retirement, skimped out on my pension as punishment for keeping things from them. I made a few shoddy investments and have been living on next to *nothing* since. June, please, you have to believe me—"

A loud crash from the front hallway halts his plea.

"What in the blazes—" Dr Cooke jumps out of his chair.

My grandfather appears in the doorway, wearing his striped pyjamas— including the bottoms, thank God— with his slippers. His eyes lock onto Dr Cooke.

"You bloody rat bastard!" the Professor yells before lunging towards his old friend, his hands up and grabbing Dr Cooke around the neck.

"Professor, no!" I yell, trying to help Dr Cooke pry the Professor's hands off from around his throat.

"You ruined my life!" he yells, tightening his grip.

"I— dob—" Dr Cooke tries to answer but it comes out in a garbled mess.

"Professor, please, stop!" I plead with him, pulling with all my might on his arm but it won't budge.

Suddenly Griffin joins the fray and together we are able to pull the Professor away. I fall backwards into a heap on the floor, my glasses slipping to the end of my nose.

I look up to see Griffin's arms around the Professor's chest, restraining him.

"You are honestly the worst care provider I have ever met!" I yell at him as I get back on my feet. "Your one job was to make sure he stayed in the car!"

"I was scouting the perimeter!" he yells in defence. "I was making sure no one was getting ready to attack."

"Cocked that one up, I'd say," Dr Cooke says, rubbing his throat.

"Well, does he know where it is?" Griffin asks me, ignoring Dr Cooke's remark.

"Don't believe anything that rat bastard tells you June, it's all lies!" The Professor says.

"What do I know about what?" Dr Cooke asks, looking from Griffin to me.

I study his face, watching his reaction very carefully.

"They've found the Shield of Quell," I reveal, and watch as his eyes widen in fear.

"Impossible," he breathes, looking from me to the Professor. "The Shield does not exist."

"We finally agree on something," the Professor says, and stops struggling against Griffin's grip.

"You've seen it?" Dr Cooke asks, turning to me. "You've seen the Shield?"

I nod. "It looked genuine; it's been authenticated. I'm guessing by your shock that you were not one of the historians they asked to validate the piece?"

"I have never seen the Shield," he says, his back straight. "Not twenty years ago, and certainly not recently. And I'll have it on record that I've never once said anything to the contrary."

"Relax, there are no cameras here to prove your innocence," I say. I'm still quite unsure as to whether I believe the innocent act that he is so adamantly playing.

"But…" Dr Cooke shakes his head, looking utterly confused. "I just don't understand. Where has it been all this time?"

"I think the better question is, who found it, and when?" I look to the Professor, knowing that the answers to those questions are what will determine his freedom.

Chapter Eleven

Griffin loosens his grip on the Professor and when he doesn't bolt towards Dr Cooke, Griffin seems mollified that he won't attack the man again.

"I need a bloody drink," the Professor says, collapsing in the green wingback chair and holding his head in one hand.

"I have some scotch in the kitchen," Dr Cooke says, and disappears into the other room.

I realise that now isn't the time to bring up the conflict with the alcohol and the Professor's medication. I think I might need a drink as well.

"If he thinks I'll ever forgive him, he's a bloody fool," the Professor says, his eyes carefully watching the now empty doorway.

I look at him, seeing the struggle in his expression. It's not just about the loss of his career, I realise. He lost his best friend, too.

"I don't know what I hoped to achieve coming here," I sigh. "He hasn't seen the Shield. He was as shocked as I was when he heard the Shield actually exists. I'd hoped he had seen it, that he had somehow authenticated it falsely to save his own neck, but he didn't."

"Of course he didn't see it! No self-respecting historian would authenticate that piece," the Professor says as Dr Cooke comes back in the room. "Or is calling you a self-respecting historian giving you too much credit, Daniel?"

Dr Cooke's hand falters slightly. He places the tray he carried from the kitchen down on the table, the glasses filled with amber liquid.

"Albert, how many times are you going to make me apologise?"

"Every second of every bloody day wouldn't be enough!" the Professor yells, causing Griffin to take a step closer to him, obviously preparing to restrain him again.

"I tried to save you. For years I covered up your mistakes, your delusional ramblings. You're not the only one who lost their career, Albert!"

The Professor starts to rise from his chair again so I quickly stand in between the two men with my arms raised.

"Stop it! Both of you," I say, shooting the Professor a warning glance. "This isn't getting us anywhere."

The Professor narrows his eyes at Dr Cooke, but lowers himself back into the chair.

"So where does that leave us?" Griffin asks. "If he hasn't seen the Shield, he can't tell you if it is a fake. Which means it could be real and those people won't stop coming after us."

"What people?" Dr Cooke's gaze darts to me. "Why are people coming after you?"

"We don't even know if they are…" I look from Griffin to Dr Cooke. "What I mean is—"

"The Shield has been stolen and the Ashmolean is under the impression that we are the ones who nicked it," the Professor says, matter of factly. "Are those drinks for us, Daniel?"

"They think—" Dr Cooke's eyes widen in fear as he looks from the Professor to me. "No— not again. You have to leave, immediately!"

He picks up the tray and starts to walk back to the kitchen.

"We haven't stolen anything!" I say, stepping in front of him to block his way.

"How could you?" he accuses. "How could you come here?"

"How could I? I came here because I needed answers and I think after all these years that's the least that you owe us," I answer.

His chin shakes a little, his lips draw tightly together and I hear the tray rattle as he studies my face. I stare into his eyes, trying to control all the pain and anger that must be clouding my own.

"Fine," he finally replies. "Ten more minutes. I'll answer whatever you want to know, and then you leave."

The Professor reaches his hand in between us and takes one of the glasses filled with scotch off of the tray.

"I need to know everything you know about the Shield,"

116

I say.

Dr Cooke looks at the Professor's face as though he would prefer not to have this conversation in front of him. I shake my head, letting him know that I don't plan on letting the Professor out of my sight again. Dr Cooke nods once before walking back to the settee.

"I don't know much. There aren't a lot of facts about any of the unfound pieces, just historians' guesses," he says, placing the tray on the table in front of him before sitting down again. "You obviously know about the Anglo-Saxons and King Raedwald."

"I know a fair bit," Griffin interrupts from beside me.

I turn my head slowly to look at him.

Dr Cooke continues, "King Raedwald was the King of East Angles for the first half of the seventh century; he ruled over what we presently know as Norfolk and Suffolk—"

"Where the ship was buried," Griffin points out, and then looks pleased he was able to make the connection.

"Precisely," Dr Cooke nods before continuing. "We don't know a great deal about the man. The Viking invasions in the ninth century destroyed most of the monasteries in East Anglia where many of the documents were kept. But what we do know suggests that he was one of the greatest Kings we have in our history books. One who shaped much of the world we live in today."

"And the Shield, it belonged to this King Raedwald, right?" Griffin asks.

"Precisely, my boy. He gave it to his son as a gift," the Professor interjects, "at the battle of the River Idle. The battle where his son ultimately lost his life."

"The Shield of Quell, that's what you keep calling it," Griffin says, turning to me. "Why is it named that?"

"To understand the Shield, you must first understand what led the King to give it to his son. In the early seventh century a boy was born named Edwin. Edwin lived most of his childhood in exile from his home of Northu, the reason still inconclusively known to historians, but what we do know is that the King of Northu, Ethelfrith, wanted it this way. No one knows for certain what the King of Northu's relationship was to Edwin, but he is rumoured to be his older brother. We know little more about Edwin's childhood, but in 610 AC he married the king of Cearl's daughter and came under the protection of King Raedwald," Dr Cooke explains. "Ethelfrith was furious that Edwin evaded his exile, and went to Raedwald to have Edwin killed. He offered Raedwald money and riches, but Raedwald refused. Ethelfrith sent two more messengers; both to encourage Raedwald to kill Edwin or war would descend on his lands. By the third messenger it is believed that Raedwald had changed his mind and decided to kill Edwin."

"Bloody typical," the Professor interjects, taking another sip from his glass. "The first chance of trouble and he betrays his friend."

Dr Cooke's jaw tightens.

"Albert, you know better than anyone else that he didn't end up betraying Edwin." Dr Cooke frowns at his old friend

"What happened?" Griffin ignores the tension between the two men and leans forward.

I try not to look at him annoyed, though to be honest it's a little difficult. He wasn't this interested when I was telling him the story.

"A chance arose for Edwin to flee Raedwald's kingdom. He knew what was about to transpire; King Raedwald had agreed to hand him over. Edwin, however, stayed. He owed his loyalty to Raedwald, and chose to see it through until the end," the Professor answers Griffin's question

"That is some historian's interpretation," Dr Cooke admits.

"Because it's the truth," the Professor interjects.

Dr Cooke looks at the Professor, irritation clear on his face. "May I?"

The Professor holds out his hands, indicating for him to continue.

"King Raedwald was married and they had a son together, Raegenhere, whom he loved dearly. After the third messenger had left with Raedwald's promise that Edwin would be given to Ethelfrith, Raedwald's wife approached her King and admonished him for cowering to his enemies. She convinced him that a real King bowed to no one, and could never be bribed with gold. So Raedwald declared war and set off with his soldiers to the Battle of the River Idle."

"And Raedwald won the Shield at the battle?" Griffin asks, hanging onto every word.

"No, Raedwald presented it to his son before the battle. When he was told of his son's death, he ordered the Shield to be buried with him."

"I still don't think I quite understand why it's called the Shield of Quell," Griffin says.

"The Battle of the River Idle was not a war of two kings disagreeing over a nobleman, it was a far greater battle over who would lead the Anglian people. The battle re-established Christianity, it set military precedent over the land, our laws, our governing systems. All these things stem from that war," Dr Cooke says, amazement clearly evident in his voice. "It is called the Shield of Quell for what it represents. Quell, by definition, means to subdue or silence; the victory of the River Idle put an end to the struggle of governing power. Raedwald lost his son that day, but respectfully gained his Kingdom."

We all sit, mulling over what we have just heard. The only noise in the room comes from the Professor as he slowly sips his scotch.

"And you saw it?" Dr Cooke's face is filled with awe. "You actually *saw* the Shield of Quell."

"I think so," I nod, staring at a small hole in the carpet. "Right before it was stolen."

"But it must have been guarded?" his tone turns perplexed.

"It was," I say, trying not to laugh at the irony. "I was the one guarding it."

"What?" The Professor's head lifts up from studying his drink. "You knew about its existence and didn't tell me?"

"I didn't know about anything before tonight!" I argue. "I was asked to join the Alliance and our first mission was to protect the Shield."

"The what?" Dr Cooke asks.

I look from him to the Professor. I know I'm not meant to talk about it, but I think it's safe to say I have been sacked from the Alliance, so what does it matter?

"The Alliance. It's one of Oxford's secret organizations that protects priceless artefacts," I explain.

The Professor looks at Dr Cooke in confusion before they both throw their heads back, roaring with laughter.

"What's so funny?" I ask, looking from one to the other. "You don't think I'm good enough to be asked to join?"

Neither of them have stopped laughing, in fact, the Professor has grabbed his side from the pain.

"I'll have you know I graduated the top of my class at Oxford! I am a well-respected teacher, who happens to know a great deal about ancient artefacts!"

Dr Cooke is actually crying now.

"I have an eidetic memory which is unsurpassed in this country!" I stand and put my hands on my hips. "Test me on anything! Go on!"

The Professor's chuckles begin to subside and he wipes

the tears from his eyes.

"Oh June Bug, no one is questioning your abilities," his tone tries to mollify me. "What we are questioning is your so called secret 'Alliance'."

"Secret Alliance!" Dr Cooke manages to repeat the words before another spasm of laughter knocks him back.

"There is a secret Alliance!" I say, scowling at both of them. "I was recruited... I had to go through tests!"

"Was one to measure the circumference of your head to see how thick you are?" Dr Cooke chokes out before slapping his knee repeatedly.

Griffin chuckles from beside me and I narrow my eyes at him in warning.

"What? That was funny," he shrugs.

I clench my jaw in outrage. "There are multiple references to the Alliance in the Oxford library; I've read newspapers alluding to their organization," I argue. "They date back centuries."

"Who was your recruitment officer? Indiana Jones?" Dr Cooke howls.

Griffin snorts with laugher, but quickly covers his mouth and nose with his hand.

"Charles Bringlett," I say, tilting my chin up.

"That git," Dr Cooke says, shaking his head and turning to the Professor. "I still have no clue how he managed to pass your Ancient Artefacts class."

"Charles is my friend!" I argue. "And it's not just me.

There are others in the Alliance, too!"

"My dear, I've been a scholar of Oxford for the better part of fifty years, and I have never once even heard a whisper of this secret Alliance," Dr Cooke offers me a consolatory smile. "Albert?"

"I'm afraid you've been led down the rabbit hole, June Bug," the Professor says, standing and walking over to the tray for another drink.

"Right, well, this really has been a pleasure," Dr Cooke says, slapping his hands to his knees. "But, I'm afraid that's all I know about the Shield."

"I need more than that!" I argue. "I've heard the story of King Raedwald my whole life, I need more information than just a history lesson."

"I don't know anything else," Dr Cooke shakes his head in exasperation.

"You and the Professor are the only people who were in the tomb that day. I need to know exactly what the markings on the ground looked like."

"It was over twenty years ago, June," Dr Crooke says. "You're better off looking at the pictures than relying on our memory."

We both look at the Professor as he carefully sips his drink.

"The pictures in the papers are blurred, I can't make out enough detail to compare to the markings I've seen on the Shield," I say, picking up my knapsack from beside me. "I have the Professor's journals, but I can't seem to find anything specific. There are no details, no original pictures except his drawing."

I hold them out for Dr Cooke to look at, but he looks at the journals as though touching them will scorch his hands. As he shakes his head at them, I lower them onto my lap.

"All of the pictures that we took would be in our notes; files kept at the university. They're stored in the library," he says.

"I can't go to the university," I argue. "Everyone is looking for us. I'm sure they are bound to notice if I saunter up and ask to see your old files about the Shield."

"I'm sorry June," he says, "I can't help you."

"You have to," I plead, clutching the journals in my hands. "We have no one else!"

The sound of a small explosion at the front of the house causes everyone to jump, and I cover my head expecting debris to fall around me. Stomping feet are coming down the hallway and I realise the sound must have come from someone breaking down the front door.

"What the devil—" Dr Cooke says, standing.

In the doorway, blocking the only exit from the room, stands Tobias, Ciara directly behind him.

"See, this is why I was checking the perimeter," Griffin says to me.

"We just want the Shield," Tobias says, looking directly at me. "I've been instructed to get it and leave. Give it to me now, and no one will ever know you took it."

"Tobias, you have to listen to me. I don't have the Shield," I say, shaking my head.

A bored look crosses Tobias's features, as though my denial was exactly what he expected.

"It's true, she doesn't have it," Griffin asserts, aligning his body to block me from Tobias's glare. I would be semi-flattered if I didn't know the only reason he is protecting me is because he needs me to testify for him.

"Even if she did have it, it would be bloody worthless," the Professor sniffs before downing the last bit of his drink.

"Tobias, please, I know you don't know me, but I'm telling you the truth," I implore him to believe me. "If I could just speak to Charles—"

"I know exactly who you are, June," Tobias says, his high cheekbones clenching as he speaks. "You aren't the only one who did their homework."

"What do you mean?" I frown.

"This wouldn't be the first time you've taken something that doesn't belong to you," he says, and my eyes widen in surprise.

"June wasn't even at Sutton-Hoo," the Professor argues.

"I'm not talking about the Shield," Tobias says.

"That's a bloody lie!" The Professor yells. "The Jensons are not thieves!"

"What has Charles said to you?" I ask, shocked at the implication.

Tobias looks at the Professor, then takes in the rest of the people in the room before answering my query.

"It doesn't matter," he says, crossing his large arms over his chest, a chest that seems to be made of pure stone. "I'm only here for the Shield."

"Well, you've come a long way for nothing, then!" I argue and watch as the vein protrudes on the top of his shaved head. "It was you that broke into my house earlier this evening, wasn't it?"

His crystal blue eyes narrow and I have my answer.

"I hope you know you were trespassing! I should call the police and press charges!"

"I have to admit I was fooled," Tobias says to me. "I would have sworn you were shocked when the Shield was unveiled."

"I *was* shocked!" I argue.

"I saw that security case myself," he shakes his head. "You had to have been planning that heist for weeks. The underpants were a nice touch, by the way," he nods towards the Professor.

"Tobias, please, you have to believe me. I didn't take the Shield," I say, pleading with him.

"We've already looked like fools once today. Don't make this harder than it has to be," he says while Ciara shuffles her weight from one foot to the other behind him.

I throw my arms up in exasperation. "What do you want from me?" I yell. "I can't give you something I don't have!"

He studies my face, watching as I try and calm the frustration that shakes through my body. Finally, he nods.

"Okay," he says.

"What?" I stand up straighter.

My mind quickly plays over the exchange and I can't help but feel like I am being led into something here.

"Sure," he shrugs, uncrossing his arms and moving his hands to his waist. "You can come with us and tell the police you haven't taken it. We will get this all sorted out."

Griffin puts his hand on my arm. "I don't think so."

"Wouldn't an innocent person *want* to clear their name?" Tobias tilts his head, and I can tell he's goading me.

My eyes skip over to the Professor and I see he is starting to doze off in the chair amidst all the chaos. I look back at Tobias, weighing my options. My first instinct through this entire evening has been to run, but maybe this whole time I have just been creating an air of doubt around myself. Tobias is right. I should go to the police station. I don't have the Shield, and the sooner everyone knows that, the better.

Making my decision I nod and step towards him.

"Alright, nobody move!" Griffin reaches into his back pocket and pulls out a gun. He points it straight at Tobias.

I look at the piece of metal in his hand and am completely dumbfounded.

"What are you doing?" I hiss at him, looking at the gun in shock. "You're only making things worse!"

"They can't *get* any worse, June," Griffin shakes his head.

"You honestly think this guy is planning to take you to the police station?"

"We haven't done anything wrong," I try to reason with him. "You are making us look guilty!"

He ignores my words and instead looks at Dr Cooke.

"Do you have a cellar?" he asks him.

"My boy, does it look like this house has a bloody cellar?" He laughs. "I'm lucky I have room for a bed."

"Well, what room can we lock them in?" Griffin forces his tone to be patient.

"I've got a pantry," Dr Cooke shrugs.

Griffin slowly closes and opens his eyes, sighing heavily.

"Pantry it is," he nods.

"No one is going in the pantry!" I yell, reaching for Griffin. "Griffin, I can't run anymore. I need to go with them so everyone can see I don't have the Shield."

"And you think they are just going to accept your word for it, and let you go on your way? We can't leave it like this, not yet," he looks at me as though my idea is ludicrous.

"Oh, I'm sorry, are we rushing things too much for you? Don't think you have enough material yet to be rich and famous?"

He frowns at me before shaking his head.

"You don't get it, June. They don't give a toss if you have the Shield or not! They are going to frame you, just like they've been doing to the Professor all along!"

I study Griffin, trying to determine if he really believes

what he is saying or if he is just using this as an excuse to draw things out. He seems genuinely concerned, but I just can't be sure. I look over at Tobias, who hasn't taken his eyes off of me. There is something about the rigidness of his stance that makes me doubt his assurance that he is going take me to the police station. Griffin's words bounce around in my head and I start to doubt the decision to give myself up.

Griffin raises his eyebrows to Dr Cooke. "The pantry?"

"It's just behind you," Dr Cooke says, pointing to a closed door.

"Right, open it," Griffin orders Ciara by pointing the gun at her.

"You be careful with dat!" Ciara says. She turns around and tries to open the door to the pantry but the handle is stuck. After a few forceful pulls, the door swings open.

"Mind the mess!" Dr Cooke says as a bucket falls off one of the shelves.

"Now both of you get in there and shut the door," Griffin orders.

A vein on Tobias's forehead throbs at Griffin's command, but he looks down at the gun that Griffin holds steady and bites back whatever it is he wants to say. He looks at me, our eyes lock, and I see the silent warning that this isn't over.

Ciara walks into the pantry, moving the broom and mop that lean against a small stool on the floor. Tobias follows, though he is barely able to wedge his body through the narrow doorway.

Griffin walks over and shuts the door.

"Not a move!" Griffin yells to them.

Putting his ear to the door, Griffin listens to the silence on the other side before nodding and taking a step backwards, his gun still pointing at the closed door. 'Right, June help Dr Cooke move the settee out into the hall here."

I nod and take the far end, and Dr Cooke takes the other. We somehow manage to squeeze it through the doorframe.

"Mind the fabric!" Dr Cooke warns. "This is a family heirloom."

"Professor, if you could come into the hallway," Griffin instructs.

The Professor looks up from his notebook.

"Writing your memoirs, Albert?" Dr Cooke says, wiping the sweat off of his forehead.

"Just reminding myself you're still missing your spine," the Professor snipes back, closing the notebook and putting it back in the breast pocket of his pyjamas. "In case I forget later."

Once we are all in the hallway with the couch we look at Griffin. No one is quite sure what to do next.

"We are going to jam the door shut with the settee wedged in between the walls," he explains, handing me the gun. "Hold this, will you?"

I look down at the metal piece in my hand, my eyes

widening. It's much lighter than I thought it would be, actually.

With Dr Cooke's help, Griffin manages to wedge the couch under the door handle.

"Right, that's not going anywhere," he nods towards the closet. "And neither are they."

"We need to leave," I say to him. "We will have to take Dr Cooke with us."

"We most certainly bloody do not!" the Professor says, shaking his head. "I'm not sitting in a car with that traitor!"

"Professor, we need his help," I try and reason with him. "We can't leave him here, what if he calls the police?"

"I won't," Dr Cooke promises, crossing his heart with his finger. "Albert's right, I don't need to go with you. If anything, my involvement will only cause more suspicion."

"Suspicion for us, or for you?" I ask him.

"We are all going," Griffin says, taking the gun back from me and putting it in his back pocket. "And I suggest we leave now."

Griffin offers a smile before he takes a hold of Dr Cooke's arm and leads him to the front door.

"Oh, and they've only gone and broke my bloody door in!" Dr Cooke yells, pointing at the remains of the wooden door in his front hallway. "That will cost me a fortune to replace."

"Isn't that a shame," the Professor smiles as he walks over the broken splinters of wood.

Chapter Twelve

"Where did you get that gun?" I scold Griffin, hitting him on the arm once we are outside. "What are you doing with a *gun*?"

"Ouch," he says, grabbing his arm where I hit it. "Relax, it's not real."

"What?"

"It's not real," he repeats, taking it out of his back pocket. "It's a prop from one of my plays."

I look from the gun to Griffin's face in bewilderment. "Why do you have a fake gun?"

"I drive a taxi for a living. I never know what crazies I'm likely to meet. Case in point," he gestures to me. "I got it out of my glove box while I was doing my surveillance earlier."

"*I'm* the crazy one?" I ask, putting my hand to my chest. "What if they knew it was a fake?"

He looks down at the gun as a tiny shadow of doubt crosses his features.

"Well, they didn't," he says, as though the argument is moot.

"Unbelievable," I mutter before brushing past him.

As I'm about to reach the car, my mobile rings from inside my knapsack. I whip it off my back and scramble in the front pocket for the phone.

"June, no, it's not a good idea," Griffin says, trying to reach for the phone, but I quickly turn my back to him and bring the phone to my ear.

"Charles?" I ask.

"June?" I hear Max's voice. "Oh thank God you're alright. Listen, Tobias and Ciara are on their way to Dr Cooke's house. You need to leave before they get there."

"Yes, I know, they've already arrived," I say, looking back at the house.

"They have? Are you alright?" he asks.

"Yes, I'm fine. I've locked them in the pantry," I explain. "Max, I need to speak to Charles."

"I– I don't think that is going to be possible," Max hesitates.

"What do you mean? I need to tell him to stop this!"

"June, Charles is on the war path here. He received a call shortly after you left the Ashmolean and he started screaming that it wasn't his fault," Max pauses for a moment. "He hung up and then immediately ordered Tobias and Ciara to go and bring you back to the museum."

"What?" I say, shaking my head. "Why would he do that? He knows I don't have the Shield."

"June, the Alliance is not taking the Shield's disappearance lying down. They want it back. The museum wants it back. Everyone is walking around here blaming everyone else… though now they seem to have all banded together and are placing the blame on Charles," he says. "He's… not handling this very well. I think Charles might be starting to believe that you have it."

"He would never," I argue. "If I could just *talk* to him…"

"June, he doesn't know I am calling you," Max admits. "He doesn't know I have been helping you. When he finds out Tobias and Ciara have failed again…"

"What about the reporters?" I ask, suddenly remembering running from the museum because of their imminent arrival. "What did Charles tell them?"

"I don't think they suspected anything was wrong. Though they didn't have much to go on. Charles just said the museum had acquired a new piece and were testing the alarms. They have no clue what to expect at the Gala."

"The Gala is still on?" I ask in bewilderment.

"Charles thinks he still has time to find you– to get the Shield back," Max corrects himself quickly.

"Why are you helping me?" I ask. Looking over my shoulder, my eyes meet Griffin's, who's tapping his finger on the face of his watch, telling me to hurry up.

"I like you June, you were really nice to me when I took that class. I know you have hundreds of students, but, well, I felt encouraged by you, by the way you cared for your grandfather. My grandfather raised me as well, so I know what you are feeling– how you just want to protect him. My grandfather admired the Professor and his work, he never believed what they accused him of," he says and I can tell he is searching for the right words to explain. "I don't believe you did this."

I grip the phone tighter, my eyes smarting with tears. I didn't realize how much I needed to hear that right now. It seems like I have been repeating myself, over and over again, and it's nice to finally have someone adamantly deny my involvement in this.

"Can't they just check the cameras? Charles said every angle is covered. Everyone could *see* I didn't do this."

"The security cameras were down– God only knows how– I'm working on trying to restore them. I hate to say this June, but Charles really cocked this one up. The Shield's casing wasn't even armed yet. When I went down to talk to the security guard about the systems he barely knew what a router was. You should have seen his face when the alarm went off; he looked petrified and kept asking me if I knew what to do. He's the night guard for the whole museum, for Christ's sake!" Max says, and I can hear something in the background. "June, someone is coming. I have to go."

"Will you call me again?" I ask, clutching the phone to my ear.

"I'll call you in the morning; it should be enough time for me to restore the camera footage. In the meantime, take out the battery and sim card in your phone. It's how they have me tracking your location."

"What should I do?" I say, my gaze focusing on the Professor, who has his back purposefully turned to Dr Cooke.

"Don't do anything. Just go somewhere safe, somewhere no one would expect you to go," he says, his voice turning to a whisper. "June, I have to go."

"Wait! Max?"

"Yes?" he asks.

My voice falters and I turn away from the men looking at me. "Thank you," I whisper into the phone before I disconnect.

I take the battery and chip out of my phone. I'm careful to put all the pieces into my bag before opening the front passenger door and sliding into the seat.

The men open their doors, all getting into the car without saying a word as I wipe the tears off my cheeks.

"Er– what was that about?" Griffin says, nodding to the knapsack and my discarded phone.

"It was my friend, the one who is helping me," I say, distracting myself by putting my seatbelt on. "He told me to shut off my phone. It's how they've been tracking me."

"Have they found the Shield?" Dr Cooke asks, leaning forward from the backseat.

"No," I say, shaking my head. "The security cameras were down, so they still don't know anything. My friend is working on fixing them now."

"And Charles?" Griffin asks.

"He's sending them after me." I lower my head.

"That spineless git," the Professor says, shaking his head.

"He's just doing his job," I argue from the front seat. "He's lost the priceless artefact that he was supposed to be guarding. He's terrified."

And from the sounds of things he could be in a lot of trouble himself, but I decide not to tell them this.

"So that makes it okay that he is throwing you to the wolves?" Griffin asks, raising his voice.

"Hear, hear!" the Professor agrees from the back seat.

"No," I concede. I look up to meet Dr Cooke's eyes in the rear-view mirror. "But he's losing everything and doesn't know what to do."

"So what now, then?" Griffin asks, looking past me to the broken front door of Dr Cooke's house, and obviously thinking of the occupants in the pantry.

"Max said we should go somewhere that no one would think to look for me," I bite my bottom lip, wracking my brain for such a place. "I have no idea where that would be, though."

Griffin thinks for a minute before snapping his fingers and turning the ignition of the car. "I know just the place."

He switches the meter on before putting the car into gear, and it takes everything inside of me to not make a comment about it.

Once we are safely on the motorway, Griffin cautiously

looks over at me.

"I feel like maybe we should just address the elephant in the car," he hedges.

"I just had something in my eye," I say, wiping my face again. "It's not a big deal."

"Actually, I was talking about the big prat in the pantry saying you've stolen something *else*," Griffin clears his throat, looking even more uncomfortable now.

"I've never stolen anything in my life," I argue.

"Hey, I believe you," Griffin says, raising his hand. "I'm just saying, it's a little strange how in one day you've been accused of nicking something twice."

"Charles misplaced some money a few years ago, and his parents accused me of stealing it," I explain, trying not to make a big deal about it.

"How much money?" he asks.

"Two-hundred thousand pounds."

Griffin swerves across the lane at my words.

"I wouldn't describe that as *some* money!" he argues. "How does someone lose that kind of money?"

"The bank said it was a glitch in his account," I shrug "It was returned, and everything was fine. Charles hadn't even noticed it was gone. His mother was the one who called and told him it was missing."

I remember the exact day it happened. Charles had come into the lecture hall where I was teaching one of the Professor's classes. He was worried about the lost money and wanted me to help him figure it out by looking over his bank statements to see where it could have gone, but I couldn't. That was the same day the article had come out about Dr Cooke's betrayal, and the Professor was a mess. I couldn't leave to help Charles; I had to make sure the Professor was all right.

Griffin shakes his head. "I will never understand rich people. How can you not know two-hundred thousand quid is missing from your bank account?"

"Normally I would agree with you, but you just have to know Charles," I say, searching for a way to explain. "He's careless. He leaves his bank statements lying around his house. He has his national insurance number written on a post-it that's pinned up on a board in his office."

"Alright, so the idiot found out his money was missing. How did you get mixed up in all of it?"

"His parents have never exactly been warm towards me. I think they thought I had my eyes set on Charles for his money. And then there was the stain on the family name... Well, they didn't exactly approve of the connection."

"So they just flat out accused you of stealing the money?"

"They subtly hinted. I think they brought my memory for numbers into it," I say. "But Charles wouldn't hear of it. He never wavered in his defence of me and he never has. Then the money was returned, and everything was fine."

"Where was it, though?" Griffin presses.

"The bank just claimed it was an error. The money was back within a fortnight. Once he had it back, I don't think Charles really cared, to be honest," I admit.

"And this is the mastermind they have leading your Alliance?" Dr Cooke chuckles from the backseat.

"Charles may be careless, but it doesn't mean he isn't smart," I argue. "Besides working at the museum part time, he also helps run his family's furniture business and it's very successful."

"How does one sell dining sets wrong?" Dr Cooke frowns.

"Let me get this straight: the man who's in charge of a secret Alliance to guard priceless artefacts had two-hundred thousand quid missing from his account a few years ago and didn't even blink an eye about it?"

"Well, he was *concerned*," I argue.

Griffin continues as though he didn't hear me. "You know, I bet that Shield would have cost quite a bit of money to buy…" Griffin says to us with raised eyebrows. "Does no one else see a connection here?"

"He didn't buy the Shield of Quell," I argue. "For one, the money that was missing from his account was returned!"

"What if he just needed the money to buy it? You said it yourself that the money was only missing for a short time. What if he bought the Shield, and then sold it to someone else?"

"The Shield would collect much more than two-hundred

thousand pounds on the black market," I argue.

"Unless the bloody fool didn't know what he was selling," the Professor suggests.

"And then what? The Shield just happened to reappear in the exact same museum where he works?" I ask in disbelief. "That's a pretty big coincidence."

"Unless it isn't a coincidence at all!" Griffin says, obviously keen on the theory. "What if that was a part of the deal when he sold it. That the Shield would have to be donated to the museum when Charles decided it was the right time."

"Why would someone buy it on the black market only to turn it over to the museum?" I ask.

"I don't know– maybe the love of history like you are always on about," Griffin says in exasperation. "Does it matter? This clears your name!"

"How?" I frown. "There's absolutely no proof that Charles, or anyone else, bought or sold that shield. All we have is your speculations."

I wish it were that simple, but without any way of proving who bought or donated the Shield to the museum, we are back to square one again. We're all silent as we try and process what we know.

"So what are we going to do then?" Griffin asks.

"I don't know. Go somewhere that Tobias and Ciara won't be able to find us. Lay low until I hear from Max again," I answer.

"And what am I supposed to do?" Dr Cooke asks from the backseat. "Those two hired thugs are in my pantry! It may never be safe for me to go home again!"

"They are only after the Shield," I try and reason with him. "Once this is all sorted you'll never hear from them again."

"That's another thing," Griffin frowns. "What exactly are those two qualified to guard?"

"What do you mean? I handpicked them myself, they're highly qualified," I argue. Though why I am defending two people who are currently trying to frame me for a crime I didn't commit is beyond me.

"I think I've seen that woman before," the Professor says, scrunching his face in thought. "Isn't she in an ad on the telly for Fanta? You know the one where she sees the little boy being bullied at the park and gives him a Fanta from her pocket?"

I offer the Professor a smile. For some reason he seems to be doing a little better in the last hour or so.

"No, Ciara lives in Ireland," I say to him. "She's a master of Capoeira, a special form of martial arts."

Griffin snorts from beside me.

"What?" I ask.

"She had trouble opening the door," he points out.

"And who is the big brute that broke my bloody door?" Dr Cooke asks from the back seat.

"Tobias is ex-MI5," I say. "He used to protect a

dignitary's family."

"An ex-MI5 agent?" Griffin repeats, the doubt obvious in his voice. "And he couldn't tell I was waving a fake gun at them?"

"I–" I search for the words. "It looked real to me!"

"And now the last member of your Alliance is trying to fix the cameras to prove you're innocent?" Griffin's eyes are wide while he shakes his head. "We'll all be in lockup before breakfast."

"Down the rabbit hole, June Bug," the Professor idly comments from the back seat before resting his head on the window.

And now that the doubts are there, they reel through my head over and over again. Nothing has felt right since the second I walked into that museum. The Shield, Charles, the Alliance. I realize that nothing may be what it seems.

"Where are we going, anyways?" I ask Griffin in hopes of changing the subject.

"A place they would never think to look for you," he offers. "My mum's."

"Your mum's?" I say frowning. "We can't go there! What if they come looking for us again? We'll be putting your mum in danger."

"They have no clue who I am," Griffin argues. "My mum doesn't live too far from here, and it will give us a chance to have a rest and a proper think about this whole thing."

"I don't like it," I say, shaking my head.

"You know, all the decisions you've made so far haven't exactly put us ahead," Griffin points out. "But if it wasn't for my quick thinking back there, you'd be in their backseat off to God knows where to be framed for a crime you didn't commit!"

I watch him carefully and begrudgingly admit that he might be slightly right.

"And you're sure she won't mind?" I ask him.

"Are you kidding? With this many people to fuss over?" Griffin smiles. "It will be the highlight of her year."

Chapter Thirteen

I stand up to put my dish in the sink only to be pushed back down into my seat.

"I'll get that, love," Ruth says, taking my plate from my hand.

"Thank you, Mrs Holt," I offer her a smile.

"I told you, it's Ruth!" she admonishes, shooting me a warning look that I quickly nod at.

Griffin's mum, Ruth, met us at the door with open arms when we arrived late in the night. Dressed in her blue quilted dressing gown and rollers wrapped tightly around her platinum blond hair, she didn't seem put off in the slightest by the unexpected guests. I don't think she gives much thought to embarrassment really, because she still has the curlers in this morning even though both the Professor and Dr Cooke have come down for breakfast. It makes me wonder if she ever plans on taking them out, and how tight those curls are going to be.

The Professor and Dr Cooke have already managed to get into a disagreement this morning over who was going to have the last blueberry scone. It was quickly resolved when Ruth told them both to shut it or they were getting it round the ear.

She quite scares me, actually.

I study the Professor over the rim of my coffee cup. He looks at Dr Cooke reading the morning paper, and I can tell he is looking for an argument. Usually I would deter him from such things, but I noticed last night and this morning that him being near his old friend has actually done him good. Of course he would never admit it himself. He took his medication this morning without any fuss; swallowing the pills while giving Dr Cooke a death stare, as though he wanted to have all his wits about him today. Whatever the motives, it was actually a nice change from the quarter of an hour argument we usually have.

"Morning, everyone," Griffin says as he walks into the room. Having just showered, his hair is dripping wet and the water is collecting on the back collar of his red shirt.

Ruth managed to fit the men into some of Griffin's dad's old clothes, though neither the Professor nor Dr Cooke is the right size. The green striped jumper she gave to the Professor sits loosely on his shoulders, the trousers secured with the shortest notch on his belt. Dr Cooke, on the other hand, is wearing a shirt that barely stretches across his belly, and leisure trousers with an elasticated waist.

I drew the line and told Ruth I wouldn't be wearing any of her clothes, choosing to just wear what I had on the night before. That's pretty much the only thing I've been able to stand my ground on under her fiery orders.

"Your girlfriend here was telling me all about your predicament," Ruth says to Griffin, kissing him on the cheek and leaving a bright red mark from her lipstick. "Right mess you've got yourself into this time."

"Girlfriend?" Griffin looks at me a little petrified.

I try and squash down the irritation the look brings me. Honestly, I'm surely not that bad.

"I've tried all morning," I say, waving his objection away. "I've learned it's just best to agree with her."

"That's my girl," Ruth says, trying to tuck some more of my hair behind my ear as she walks past.

"And what exactly were you telling Mum, honey dearest?" Griffin's tone is sweet but I can see his wide eyes staring at me, wondering what I've done.

"Nothing," I say, trying to be polite as possible. "I think that's your mum's way of trying to get you to tell her what I wouldn't."

Griffin laughs, looking at his mum fondly.

"Fell for that one or two times, haven't I, Mum?" he asks, buttering a cranberry scone.

"Certainly have, my love," she says, pulling a chair out for him beside me. "And how come you never told me you were dating such an accomplished young woman?"

She looks at me fondly but her eyes travel up to my hair and I can see the slight wince.

"Well, considering we only met last night, didn't have much time I'm afraid," Griffin sits down with his scone and tea cup.

"Her grandfather's been singing her praises all morning."

It's true, which is a bit unusual for him. I mean, I know he loves me in his own way, but I would have never called the Professor particularly *affectionate*. He wrote on my sixteenth birthday card that I was becoming exceptionally good at recognizing the difference between idea and proof in my logical formulas. That was his way of saying *I love you*. But this morning he's been telling Ruth everything I've ever accomplished. Which would be lovely... if that's all that he was doing it for. But something tells me it has more to do with the man sitting beside him than the woman he speaks of. He's trying to make it clear to Dr Cooke that we managed to succeed even without his support.

Still, he said he's always admired the persistence of the gold flecks in my otherwise plain brown eyes, so that was nice.

Griffin doesn't offer anything but a smile before taking a bite of his scone.

"So..." Ruth sits down across the table beside Dr Cooke, looking from Griffin to me.

"So?" Griffin asks between mouthfuls.

"So..." she asks, raising her hands at the two of us.

"Mum..." Griffin warns before giving me a look that clearly says that this is *my* fault.

"What? Is it too much for me to ask to finally have you

settled?" she asks, and I swear from her tone she's working on some tears. "Your father– God rest his soul– and I didn't knock down that wall into my sewing room so you could have a bigger room just for yourself!"

I choke on my coffee, and quickly pat my chest.

"I'm not getting any younger," she squints her eyes and I'm convinced she is pinching her leg to try and make herself cry. "I want to go out and show off my grandchildren before I'm old and dead!"

I can't help my gaze as it travels to her head of curlers. Would she take those out before she took the baby out in the pram?

"We'll work on it," Griffin promises her, not even looking at me.

I look up to see the Professor studying me with a frown on his face. Not sure what is going through his head I offer him a reassuring smile, but he continues to study me.

"Did you put your laundry in the hamper?" Ruth asks Griffin. "I'm going to do a load of laundry and then pack you all a lovely lunch for your journey."

Griffin mumbles thanks through a mouth full of scone, and Ruth turns and leaves the dining room.

"So..." I say and try to keep me tone as neutral as possible. "You live with your Mum?"

Griffin stops chewing to look up at me. "So?"

"Nothing," I say, shrugging my shoulders and pretending to study the arts section of the newspaper.

"You live with your Grandfather," Griffin points to the Professor, his tone bordering on defensive.

"Oh, would we say it's the same thing?" I ask, keeping my eyes fixed on the paper.

"How is it different?" he asks, turning towards me.

"Well, the Professor isn't well," I say, turning the page.

"Neither is Mum," Griffin argues.

I look up at him with scepticism. "What's wrong with her?"

Griffin opens his mouth to answer, but nothing comes out.

I raise my eyebrows before looking back down at the newspaper again.

"She gets sick with worry!" He finally manages to spit out. "All those late nights for me, it's very hard on her nerves."

"I'm sure it is," I say, nodding.

"Exact same thing," I hear him mumble, which makes me smile.

"When *are* you two going to settle down?" Dr Cooke joyfully asks, before returning to his own paper.

Ignoring his comment, Griffin puts down the last bite of his scone.

"So, I've been thinking about everything that's happened," Griffin says. "And I think the best thing to do is come up with a solid plan of action before we go any further."

"Oh good, I thought the same thing," I say, folding the newspaper. "Shall you go first or shall I?"

"Shall I?" he says, his tone clearly annoyed.

I raise my hand for him to proceed. He puts both his hands on the table, clasps them together and leans forward in his chair.

"I've thought about this long and hard, and I think we are being set up. Like a conspiracy," he says, looking at each of our faces.

"Gee, what makes you think that?" I ask, my voice dripping with sarcasm.

"Can I finish, please?" his asks with wide eyes, and when I don't say anything he turns to look at the Professor. "It all comes back to the Shield. If you didn't get it from the tomb all those years ago, someone else did. We're running around in circles here, trying to prove whether the Shield is real."

The Professor starts to argue, but Griffin raises his hand for silence. "Let's just say for a moment, for argument's sake, that the Shield *is* real. June herself said she thought it looked legit in the case at the museum and the knob head did say he had it authenticated."

"His name is Charles—"

Griffin raises his hand again for silence. "I'm not finished," he says, clearly irritated.

I swallow the words and indicate for him to continue.

"I think we are looking at the wrong thing here. Forget about the Shield and whether it's real or not. The proper question we should be asking is who *stole* it," Griffin explains. "June, you said there were five people in the building with you: Charles, Tobias, Ciara, Max, and the security guard. One of *them* must have stolen it."

"Or there could have been someone else in the building that no one knew about," Dr Cooke says.

"It's true, who knows who could have been in the museum. I don't think it would have been very hard to slip past that security guard; he didn't really seem to know what was going on most of the time. And even if someone we know stole it, how would we ever prove it?" I shake my head. "Until Max is able to retrieve that camera footage we won't know anything. It's not like we can go back to the scene of the crime to investigate."

"So, what is *your* idea then?" Griffin asks, frowning.

"Exactly what you don't want to hear, I'm afraid. I think one way or another we verify the authenticity of the Shield. Not just to clear our names, but also because I can't live like this anymore. Not knowing... it's ruined our lives..." I look at the Professor.

"So you want to go to the University?" Griffin asks, shaking his head in disbelief. "You said it yourself, we wouldn't get a foot in the door before you're arrested."

"Unless," Dr Cooke snaps his fingers and sits up straighter, "we don't look at the university's copy of our dig notes, we look at a different copy instead."

"What do you mean? I thought you said you didn't have

the notes or photographs from the excavation?" I ask. "The photos in the paper are too grainy; I can't make out any details from them."

"It completely slipped my mind last night. When your grandfather and I were sent back to the University, all our equipment was sent back with us: the cameras, our excavation tools. A few years ago, though, they were lent out in order to render a display for tourists to see how the process of finding relics is done. I was one of the archaeologists that opened the exhibit— it's quite a remarkable display, actually. They even commissioned some impressive replicas of the riches actually found, and recreated tombs exactly how they were discovered. Copies of the original photos were put on display for the tourists to see."

The Professor and I share an uncertain look.

Shaking my head, I try and reassure him. "If I can look at those pictures, I will know if the Shield is real. Looking at the piece from the museum I could tell that the wood had deteriorated enough to put it in the right time period. The leather, the jewels, they all looked exactly how they should— just like you taught me to look at their settings and how they would have been bound. It could be a fantastic reproduction, or perhaps it's another piece from the time period that is trying to be passed off as the Shield you two *almost* discovered." I see the worried look in the Professor's eyes and I can't help but feel the exact same way. "If I can look at the pictures of the markings you saw on the floor of the tomb, I can tell you if they would line up with the Shield I saw at the Ashmolean."

I point to my temple where the image of the intricate boss of metal and jewels has been playing over and over in my mind since last night.

"Great," Griffin says from beside me. "Where are the pictures?"

"Where it all started my boy," Dr Cooke says, rising from his seat. "Sutton-Hoo."

Dr Cooke walks out of the room, leaving the Professor, Griffin, and I to sit at the table in silence.

"You don't have to come," I say to the Professor.

"The bloody hell I don't!" he argues, shifting in his chair. "You're not the only one on trial here, June, and this time I don't intend to idly sit back and take it."

I think back to my conversation with Dr Cooke at his house and wonder how much of this whole thing could have been avoided if the Professor hadn't become ill. He would have been more discreet with his doubts, surely.

All of this adds to my worries about bringing him back to the place where it all started. He's been doing so well today, and despite yesterday it has been a pretty good month for him. I worry that taking him back to the dig site will trigger another episode, and with his age and the progression of the disease, it's one he might not be able to recover from.

"I see the wheels turning, June Bug, but I'll be *fine*," he tries to reason with me. "Besides, Ruth put this belt on so bloody tight I worry these pants might never come off again."

"Mum's helpful like that," Griffin says to me.

Dr Cooke walks back into the room clasping his hands together.

"I've arranged a private viewing tonight at Sutton-Hoo," he says to us joyfully. "Apparently the owners are more than accommodating for one of their very own celebrities."

The Professor snorts in amusement.

"I'll have you know they think very highly of me there, Albert," he says, taking his seat at the table again. "They've even put my book on display with the excavation tools."

"I thought you said we were going to find out the truth about the Shield," the Professor says to me. "It seems all they've got at Sutton-Hoo is a case full of bogwash."

Dr Cooke grinds his teeth, and I decide to change the subject.

"Tonight is good, better to go when there aren't any people there," I say to Dr Cooke. "But what are we going to do until then?"

"We can stay here," Griffin suggests.

"Oh, I– umm, I'm not so sure that is such a good idea," I say, pointing to the doorway Griffin's mum left through.

Not that I'm not really appreciative of what Ruth has done for us, but it just isn't a good idea to stay here. The less people that are involved in this, the better.

"Oh, it will be fine. Mum won't mind," he says,

obviously misunderstanding my hesitation. Getting up from the chair he goes over to the doorway. "Mum! My friends and I are going to stay here and hang out today!"

"You've got chores!" She shouts back from upstairs.

Griffin's cheeks turn pink and he quickly looks at me before turning back to the doorway. "I'll do them tomorrow!" he tries to argue, rolling his eyes.

"Not likely! You'll do them today, young man!" she shouts back. "And that's quite enough cheek out of you!"

Griffin turns back to the room, looking uncomfortable. "I– um– just have a few things to do around the house. Shouldn't take long."

I nod and try my best not to smile.

"Maybe we'll go sit in the yard for a bit?" I try and suggest.

He just nods before turning out of the room into the hallway.

"Women: the main reason I never married," Dr Cooke says, picking up his plate to carry it into the kitchen.

The Professor picks up his own plate and follows Dr Cooke, leaving me alone in the room.

I walk over to the knapsack I left in the hallway the night before and look around me. I can hear Dr Cooke and the Professor arguing in the kitchen, and Griffin seems to have disappeared into one of the bedrooms upstairs. I peer up the stairs to make sure he isn't looking before I pick up the bag, slowly open the front door, and close it quietly behind me.

After I put my knapsack on I begin to walk until I'm a few blocks from the house. I constantly check over my shoulder to make sure no one is following me. When I come to a small park with a slide and swings, I put the bag down, get my phone out, and start to put the pieces back together.

I couldn't do this at the house. Mainly because I didn't want to hear all the reasons from Griffin that this isn't a good idea. Also if they really *are* tracing my calls, I want to keep a good distance from the house.

But my main reason for going so far from the house is Griffin's nagging.

Dialling the number, I click SEND and put the phone to my ear.

"Charles Bringlett," he answers on the first ring.

"Charles, it's me."

"June?" he says in disbelief. "Where the fuck *are* you?"

"I'm sure you can trace this and figure it out," I say, looking at my watch on my wrist. I saw in the movies that it takes them at least a minute before they are able to trace your call. I'm not sure if it's all bollocks, but I've really got nothing else to go on.

"June, you need to come back here, right now," Charles says. "Running is only making things worse for you."

"Did you find the Shield?" I ask.

"You know we didn't," he says.

"How would I know that? You don't honestly believe I did this, do you?"

From the silence on the other end I have my answer.

"Charles, I'm not convinced that the Shield is even real. I have to go and look at something to authenticate it. If it turns out to be a reproduction—"

"June you are wasting your time. It's been authenticated. It's the Shield from Sutton-Hoo," he argues, his patience growing thin.

"I'm not willing to accept that yet," I say, looking down at my watch. Thirty seconds gone.

"Well, you should. Because feigning ignorance isn't going to get anyone out of this mess," he argues.

I try not to laugh, considering burying your head in the sand is the thing Charles does best.

"So what? You're just going to send your thugs after me and throw me in jail? I didn't steal the Shield, Charles."

"Listen, June," Charles sighs and I can hear the exhaustion in his voice. "I just don't know what to believe. You were the only one near it… It disappeared right after you left…. You were against the Shield being here from the second you saw it, and then all of a sudden it's gone! What am I supposed to think? Could the Professor have taken it?"

"You don't think I would notice a large wooden shield tucked under his shirt as we were getting in the car?"

"Well, what the hell do you want me to do, June? I'm in a shit load of trouble here!"

"I want you to stop sending people after me! I want you to start believing I am innocent."

"I have always defended you," he shoots back.

"Yes, you always defended me when I didn't need defending," I say. "What I need is for you to defend me *now*."

"I– I don't know if I can, June," he admits.

It's like a punch in the stomach.

"Well maybe I should stop defending you too!" I shout back.

"What are you talking about?" he says.

"Everyone keeps telling me you are behind this, that you are setting me up to take the fall when you are the one that stole the Shield. I'm starting to think *that* makes sense."

"That's ridiculous," he argues.

"Is it? You and Tobias were the last ones in the room with the Shield. Maybe you two are in this together!" I accuse.

"Are you kidding me?" he asks. "Do you know how much trouble I am in?"

"You'll get a slap on the wrist. Fired at the most," I argue. "That's nothing when you factor the money you could get for the Shield from a private collector and you know it."

"June, you listen to me," he says, and I can hear the sheer anger in his voice. "Blaming other people for what happened isn't going to get you out of this. No one is going to believe those lies."

"Well, maybe I'll just see for myself," I say, pressing the END button on the phone.

Damn it– that was a minute and a half.

Chapter Fourteen

The journey to Suffolk takes a few hours from Griffin's house but apart from some bickering from the two men in the back seat, it has been a somewhat quiet trip so far.

"You know, I saw an interesting piece from the third Earl of Kent not too long ago," Dr Cooke says to the Professor. "Fascinating shoes said to belong to the old chap. They were at least two feet long."

"Wow," Griffin says from the driver's seat, nudging me with his elbow. "He must have been a hit with the ladies."

"It was all the fashion back then to have shoes that were much too long for one's foot," Dr Cooke explains, chuckling. "They were far too long to be practical."

"Men also wore corsets and tights during that time," I say to Griffin, smiling.

"Only the young noblemen," the Professor corrects me. "If you're going to recite history, June, you have to be accurate."

"You were always fascinated with historical garments when you were younger, June. I remember you playing with some dresses your grandmother had acquired," Dr Cooke remembers fondly. "Is that why you chose the Renaissance as your expertise?"

"One of them," I smile. "Most of the classes I teach are first year introductory courses though, so I cover a very broad range of history."

"Well, she couldn't bloody well continue her family's legacy with the Anglo-Saxons, could she?" The Professor bristles in his seat, the comment clearly meant to scorch Dr Cooke.

Dr Cooke seems uncomfortable for only a moment before he smiles and changes the subject. "You know, I heard a fascinating lecture on…"

"Those two," Griffin shakes his head at me from the front while Dr Cooke tries to engage the Professor in conversation. "Were they always like this? Arguing all the time?"

I look at the two men in the rear-view mirror and smile. "Yes."

Which is true, they always differed in opinions on virtually everything. Even when they were agreeing they somehow managed to argue. Although I'm not sure if the Professor will ever forgive Dr Cooke for what happened, it is nice to see him with his companion again, talking about what they both love most: history.

"You do a good job with him," Griffin says, indicating the Professor with a nod of his head. "I know it can't be easy."

"We have our good and bad days," I say to Griffin. "I'm

not quite as patient with him as I should be on the bad days."

"Is it just you two then? No one else?" he asks.

"The Professor raised me by himself. My father, his son, and my grandmother, both died before I was born."

"What about your Mum?" he asks.

"Not interested in me, I guess," I shrug my shoulders. "I don't know much about her, and the Professor was never willing to talk about it. Some sort of scandal is all he will ever say."

"Scandal? Like what?" Griffin asks, his interest peaking. The playwright in him is never far from the surface.

"Not a clue. I've looked through all the old newspapers, photo albums, his journals. There's nothing about her," I shrug. "I'm not even sure if the name I have for her is what she goes by now."

I used to worry about it when I was younger, combing through all the old newspapers. The Professor is vigilant about revealing nothing. Sometimes, though I'm slightly ashamed to admit it, I probe him while he is having one of his episodes. When he's in a delirious state I ask him questions, but even then I can't get any answers out of him when it comes to my mother.

It makes me wonder if he actually knows or even remembers.

With the two men still arguing in the back, Griffin looks at me from the corner of his eye.

"No– er– boyfriend to speak of, then?" he asks.

"No," I answer. "And it's not because I'm asexual either."

Griffin smiles.

"I'm not asexual in case that wasn't clear before," I say.

He nods.

"It's not exactly easy to have a romantic life with the Professor," I explain. "Men say they understand but when he starts taking his pants off at the dinner table it gets a bit uncomfortable."

He offers the laugh the comment was meant to bring, and I shake my head.

"To be honest, I don't really see the point in the whole love thing. It's never worked out for anyone I've known. The Professor and my grandmother bonded over their mutual love of history– she was one of the first female librarians at Oxford," I say, smiling. "But from what I have read in his journals I think they were more *fond* of each other than anything. History: that's what they loved the most. I think they married because it was the thing to do back then, well not so much for the Professor, but I'm sure that was my grandmother's motivation."

"I'm sure they loved each other in their own way," Griffin offers.

"Perhaps," I say, smiling. "My father– the complete opposite when it came to love, apparently. He was a lady's man, with bellbottoms and tight shirts. He fell in love with my mum, but died before I was born."

"Well, that sounds romantic, if a bit dark," Griffin says, and then obviously realizes how his comment came off. "Sorry, was that insensitive?"

"It's fine. From what I can tell my dad could be a right fool sometimes. I don't think he was particularly fond of monogamy, or so the Professor says, so probably not as romantic as I'd like him to have been."

"Bugger," Griffin replies.

"A marriage of love, a marriage of convenience, neither of them seems that spectacular of choices, do they? So I've just decided to give it a miss."

Griffin drives in silence for a while, and the two men have finally descended into quiet in the back seat.

"So, what about you? Any Mrs Holt waiting in the wings?"

"I'm married to my art, I'm afraid," he says, as though the loss to women is tragic. "Relationships are a lot of work, aren't they?"

I nod at him.

"It's probably why my agent says the romance is lacking in my plays," he reasons. "No offense, but your lot is a bit hard to figure out."

"We try to make ourselves seem more complicated than we actually are," I argue.

"And I've got Mum," he points out. "She's been a bit of a mess since my dad died, so she needs me to be there for her."

"Right," I nod in understanding. "Did he pass very recently?"

"1982," Griffin says.

I urge myself not to make a remark.

"Have you thought about moving out?" I ask, then carefully choose my next words. "It might be good for her; give her some space and force her to spread her wings a bit."

And to take out those curlers.

"No need," Griffin says, shrugging. "They knocked down the wall between the two bedrooms before I was born to give me a room and a nursery in one. I've got a couch set up there now, so it's basically like I've already got my own flat. Plus Mum likes the company. Well, you know how it is with the Professor."

"Right," I say, nodding.

It isn't the same thing at all.

"You know, in the Anglo-Saxon times, children used to stay within their family homes until they died, or until the daughter was married off," the Professor chimes in from the back seat. "Having said that, they also used to marry their first cousins, so to each their own."

I look straight ahead and don't make a sound.

Chapter Fifteen

"This is it?" Griffin asks as we get out of the car in the empty parking lot. "Where is everyone?"

"The last tour was at six." I look around. "I guess everyone has gone home."

Griffin looks from the empty car park to the three buildings around it, each separated by some distance.

First is the old Tramner estate, a large white colonial house that was the original home of Edith Pretty, the landowner who first commissioned the dig on her land in the late 1930's. Recently it was converted into more of a showpiece, the downstairs furnished with all period appropriate pieces that tourists can walk through and touch. I remember my class came here when I was in my A levels. I stayed home for that particular trip; it was just a year after the internal speculation began regarding the Professor and I decided it might be best if I didn't have any hands on experience with anything to do with Sutton-Hoo at that time.

"Albert, we set our tents up there, remember?" Dr Cooke points beside the house.

"You lived here?" Griffin asks.

"We camped on all our digs. They'd set up showers and toilets for us to use, but we lived off the land. Glorious times," Dr Cooke rests his hands on his stomach and looks at the Professor.

"You nicked my banana that last morning," the Professor says, which wipes the smile right off of Dr Cooke's face. "Don't think I've bloody forgotten everything."

"You lived out here for weeks?" Griffin asks as though he's having trouble picturing it.

"Months, my boy," Dr Cooke claps him on the back, deciding to ignore the Professor.

"Where is the site you excavated?" Griffin asks.

"The mound is about half a mile that way," I say, pointing to the north.

Griffin squints but obviously can't see anything in the dark.

Next to the house is the café, a place to eat and enjoy the scenic views of Sutton-Hoo while overlooking the River Deben. It's closed now for the evening.

Off in the distance, about a quarter kilometre away, is the building we are looking for: the Exhibition Hall.

Griffin seems uncomfortable with the lack of people; he shifts from foot to foot.

"I think it's usually this quiet at night," I try to reassure him.

"I don't like it, June Bug, not one bloody bit," the Professor pipes in, his eyes darting around in all directions.

"Where is the *security*?" Griffin shakes his head. "Aren't they supposed to have priceless artefacts here?"

"Well, the security guard will be inside," I point to the grey structure that looks like a big barn. "And there are only replicas here right now. When the genuine relics were here, the security was around the clock, but when they were given to the museum for permanent storage they obviously cut back."

"*Cut back*?" Griffin's eyes widen at the complete open space that surrounds us.

"Sutton-Hoo is over ninety-one hectares large," I argue. "Most of this is all funded by donations and run by volunteers. It would take an army to guard every square inch day and night."

"So what about the mounds you were talking about?" Griffin changes the subject and looks off into the distance again.

"They've all been re-covered," I explain. "People walk amongst them every day on tours or self guided."

"I still say it makes no sense," Griffin shakes his head. "I mean, you said that not all the mounds have been uncovered right? So there could be thousands of shields under there for all you know. You think the history police would want to stop anyone from just coming with a shovel and digging."

"They do have *some* security– ground patrols, surely?" I look to Dr Cooke, who just shrugs like he has no idea.

"No wonder all of their stuff keeps getting nicked," Griffin says, then puts his hands in his pockets as the wind picks up.

"Right, maybe we should save the details until we get inside?" Dr Cooke says to me, trying to signal the Professor and his agitated state by darting his eyes towards him.

We make our way to the tall steel building, but before we get to the door it opens and a shiny bald head pops out.

"Dr Cooke?" he asks and then shakes his head. "Don't know why I asked, I know it's you– seen your picture of course."

Dr Cooke beams at the recognition.

"Not often we get a celebrity round here," the guard smiles and reveals a large gap between his two front teeth.

The Professor snorts in amusement. Dr Cooke ignores him and offers his hand to the guard to shake.

"I spoke to someone on the phone to let them know I would like to give my friends a special, self-guided tour."

"Absolutely," he nods and eagerly opens the door wider.

The doorway opens into a small foyer with a welcome desk that is cluttered with flyers. The large entryway leads into the main section of the building.

"I've turned all the lights on for you," the guard points beyond the opening. "It does tend to be a little on the dim side though... We don't often open after hours... Of course for you it's no trouble..."

"We very much appreciate it," Dr Cooke says to the

guard.

"If it's all right with you I think I'll just nip over to the café for a snack," the guard says.

"Why not?" Griffin says from behind me, raising his arms. "I mean, we're only total strangers."

I look at him, my eyes wide, warning him to shut up.

"I wouldn't do it normally," the guard argues defensively. "But it's not likely one of you is going to nick something, is it?"

We all stare at him for a moment before laughing.

"That will be fine,' Dr Cooke says, nodding to him. "We'll let you know when we're finished. Enjoy your break."

The guard offers a small wave before walking out the door.

"Unbelievable," Griffin mutters under his breath.

As a group we walk through the archway into the main exhibit hall. The walls are lined with plaques, each dedicated to one of the mounds that were uncovered all those years ago. Below each plaque is a display case with reproduction tools and some of the priceless relics that were discovered.

"There is a small movie screen just around the corner where tourists can come watch a short documentary on some of the excavations," Dr Cooke points out. "They cut my part out, though, which is a little disappointing, as I had quite a few funny anecdotes... People love that sort of thing."

"Can't imagine why they'd cut it, you being a bloody celebrity here," the Professor says, though thankfully Dr

Cooke seems to miss the sarcasm, or chooses to ignore it.

"There's also a gift shop, somewhere," he says, turning around before shrugging. "They sell more jams than they do copies of my book– bloody uneducated lot that visits."

"Wow, they found a horse's skeleton?" Griffin asks, studying the pictures on the wall plaque. "That's cool!"

"You sound like one of our young volunteers, doesn't he, Albert?" Dr Cooke looks in the Professor's direction but my grandfather ignores the conversation. Dr Cooke waves his hand at him. "Old fuss pot."

"It must have been exciting," Griffin says, looking at the plaque with great interest. "To be able to find all of these amazing things."

I come to stand beside Dr Cooke as he looks at Griffin, smiling.

"My boy, most of the time 'exciting' is probably not the right word to describe it. Excavations of a single site can last anywhere from a few months to a few years."

"How do you know how long it will take?" he asks.

"Each dig site will have its own timeline, usually set by the lead archaeologist," I answer. "It depends on how big what they are uncovering is."

"So you just keep digging until you find the treasure, then?"

Dr Cooke laughs. "Not all of history's treasures are priceless artefacts. There are many reasons for an excavation. It's true, relics are always a hope, but the things

171

we can gain from finding different burial rituals, the resources used… all this adds up to provide 'context', which is what we draw our history from."

"I think it's mad that you haven't uncovered all the mounds," Griffin says, looking around the room.

"It's not as simple as grabbing a shovel and attacking the earth, I'm afraid," Dr Cooke explains. "Sites are only partially excavated for a variety of reasons, funding being a main one."

"It's also important for the future generations to keep sites undisturbed," I argue. "If we go around digging everything up, we won't leave any history for others to discover."

"But what if you're wrong?" Griffin replies. "What if under one of those mounds there is something that disproves everything you know about the Anglo-Saxons?"

"It's very unlikely," I say, amused. "We don't just draw our conclusions based on one relic. We rely on centuries of artefacts and knowledge gained from different sites, and all of that combined moulds our current understanding of history. But it will change, no doubt, there are new things discovered every day."

"Sounds pretty tedious," Griffin acknowledges.

"It is," Dr Cooke smiles, and turns away from the plaque. "They've recreated a tomb over here, so you can see some of the process for yourself."

Dr Cooke leads us over to the display that has been

raised from the earth. The Exhibition Hall was built around it to show the actual remains of the mound where the ship was found.

"Is this where they found the King?" Griffin asks, directing his question to the Professor, forcing him to join our group.

"This was the ship burial, and here are some of the artefacts that have been replicated from the tomb."

"There's a shield!" Griffin points excitedly to a shield in the display case, not so unsimilar in style to the Shield of Quell. "Maybe that's the one Raedwald's son used in battle."

The shield is pristine, obviously because it is a replica. The leather is in perfect condition, stretched out to the circumference of the shield. The original of this shield had to have the wood replaced because it had decayed too much over the centuries before it was discovered.

The Great Buckle and shoulder clasps are beside it, and looking at them and their precision detail I can see they're a perfect replica of the originals now on display at the Ashmolean.

"And here is our discovery," Dr Cooke says, drawing my attention to the display case off to the right.

I look at the Professor, who seems much more detached than he was in the car, and I begin to worry what this whole process is doing to his state of mind. Ignoring my concerned look the Professor walks over to the display case to peer inside.

Inside the small case is a selection of tools that I recognize as ones the Professor used to use for his excavations. The small chisel has a crack on the handle from overuse. The crowbars used to carefully open the joined woods have two prongs that are rounded and well worn. A brush with soft, limp, earth-stained bristles lies beside them.

"They've included my book, you see," Dr Cooke says to Griffin, who lifts it off the top of the glass display case where it perches on a clear bookstand. "All about our adventures, Albert."

The Professor offers Dr Cooke a stare that I am sure is a threat of severe bodily harm, so I step in front of him, my back blocking his view.

"Where are the photos, Dr Cooke?" I ask.

"Right here, my dear," Dr Cooke says, pointing to the display plaque hanging on the wall. About four feet by three feet in size, a quarter of the plaque is taken up by pictures scattered across it. The one in the top hand corner is a picture of the Professor and Dr Cooke when they first arrived at the site before the excavation began. The papers chose that picture when they wrote of the scandal.

On the middle section of the board are detailed descriptions of the tomb and the body that was uncovered inside. Believed to be a nobleman of great stature, the text alludes to his royal birth without speculating on his actual name.

At the bottom are the pictures taken of the marking,

which I immediately recognize as the ones from the papers. Unlike the papers' grainy copies, however, these pictures are bright, clear, and far larger than the ones they printed. They usually included the markings as the smallest picture on the page; the large section always reserved for the Professor's troubled face.

The first is a close up of the tomb and removed lid. Looking at the wood, it would appear that the Professor was correct in his journals: the wood did seem to be in good condition considering its age, with hardly any splitting. The lid itself was pried off in a single piece, though the blade-like markings from the crowbar scarred it greatly with two small gouges on the outer edge and two larger singular gouges a little closer to the centre.

Turning my attention to the next picture I see the tomb itself, a close up of the remains after all the soil and earth had been removed.

The last picture is the marking of the Shield, or whatever was supposedly in the tomb. Round in size, I see from the measurements of the tape measure laid out on the ground that the piece would be the same size as the shield from the museum. Looking closer at the centre markings, squinting my eyes at where the boss would have been imprinted, I see a grouping of impressions where the stones would have pressed into the ground. The first cluster's markings are small and tightly set together, almost appearing as one large indent in the ground except for the small ridges where the gems' edges left their mark in the dirt. The other groupings are comprised of larger precious stones on the Shield's boss, more distinctly impressed into the ground. I study all the markings so closely that my nose is inches away from the plaque. My eyes frantically search for one marking made by a gemstone that is out of place, anything to prove the markings aren't an exact match to the same five grape-like clusters on the Shield from the museum.

"Does it say the depth of the markings?" I ask myself, looking at the text around the pictures.

The markings measured to be 2-4 inches in depth at its deepest point. Believed to originally be the markings of a shield or large medallion.

I stand up, the dread sinking through my body at what this means.

"It was the Shield," I say, not realizing I said it out loud.

"How do you know?" Griffin almost whispers, coming to stand beside me.

"The markings, they are an exact match," I say, pointing to the picture.

He looks at the picture, clearly frustrated that he has no clue what he is even supposed to be looking at.

"So what?" he attempts to argue with me in a whispered voice. "That doesn't mean that the Professor took it. It said over there that half the mounds were empty– thieves had got there centuries before!"

"The markings wouldn't have matched up so perfectly,"

I say, shock numbing my body. "The measurements are a perfect match. If someone had stolen it years before, the ground would have settled. The depth wouldn't match."

"So what are you saying?" he asks, shaking his head. "You really think the Professor could have stolen it?"

I look over my shoulder at the Professor, who wandered off again over to the recreated excavation site.

"I don't know," I say, looking at Griffin with tears in my eyes. "Someone would have had to steal it *right* before the rest of the team looked in the tomb."

"Then that's what happened," Griffin says, not willing to contemplate any alternative. "June, if your grandfather had the Shield, you would know about it! You would have *seen* it! And how was he supposed to give it to the Ashmolean with no one having a clue it was him?"

"I don't know," I say, shaking my head, not believing that any of this is happening right now.

If you had asked me yesterday if I believed the Shield even existed I would have adamantly denied it. After I saw the Shield I thought it was just a fake, a cleverly disguised replica. Now... Now I don't know what to believe anymore.

"And who stole it from the museum?" Griffin asks, shaking his head. "Because I sure as hell don't think your grandfather could have fit it in his underpants."

I look into Griffin's eyes and suddenly I don't feel quite as doubtful as I did moment ago.

"You're right, he couldn't have stolen it from the

museum," I say. "And if he had sold it to the museum I would have known. He's never out of my sight."

"You're becoming far too predictable June," I hear Tobias's voice from behind me and I turn with a start as he and Ciara stand under the entry. "You have got to try and make this a little more challenging for me to find you."

Chapter Sixteen

"You didn't think I would find you here?" Tobias asks, rolling his eyes at my shocked expression. "We've been waiting for you to arrive all afternoon. Just had to wait for the guard to get settled on his break."

"But, I took my phone apart," I say confused.

"Charles thought you might come here," he explains, looking around at the group.

"Listen Tobias, I need to talk to Charles," I say, putting my hands up defensively. "I think the Shield might actually be real. We need to work *together* to find whoever stole it."

Tobias laughs, turning to look at Ciara. "I owe you a tenner."

"Changes her story like ya change yer pants," Ciara nods.

"She's telling you the truth!" Griffin argues.

"After spending a night in a small cramped cupboard I don't really care what story she's planning on selling us today." Tobias shakes his head, looking at Dr Cooke. "Your beans have expired, by the way."

"I know I wasn't sure before, but that was before I knew the Shield was *real*," I walk towards them and desperately try to explain. "Now I know how important it is to find the person who stole it. I want to *help* you."

"You can help us by turning yourself in," Tobias grabs my arm. "The less time I spend chasing after you, the more time I can spend looking for wherever you hid the Shield."

"What do you mean?" I ask, my arm pulled in the direction of the exit.

"I'm taking you in and then you can sing you innocence to your heart's content," he says. "I've got more important things to do."

"You're taking me to the MI5 headquarters?" I ask, flabbergasted.

I mean, they have no proof and yet they are treating me like I am already guilty!

Tobias looks over my head and shoots Ciara a worried look. "You're right, she's as batty as the old man."

"We're going to take ya somewhere safe, June," Ciara speaks as though she's talking to a child. "Somewhere ya can get help."

"I don't need help!" I say, trying to pull my arm back. "And I don't have the Shield. You're wasting precious time. Some lunatic has the Shield, and if we don't hurry it could be lost forever!"

"That's right!" Griffin yells from behind me. "She doesn't have it, because I do!"

Griffin holds up the replica shield from the display case and waves it at us before running over to the excavation display.

"He's got it!" Ciara yells, running after him before anyone has time to move, obviously unaware that the shield isn't the same one she's meant to be guarding.

She's quicker than he expected, so Griffin's eyes widen in fear before he turns to run in the opposite direction. Ciara reaches him quickly, though, and jumps to tackle his legs, causing him to fall in an ungraceful heap on the floor.

I turn around, trying to yank my arm free while Tobias is distracted, but his grip is too tight. Reaching around, I slap the side of his face with my open palm, causing his head to snap sideways.

"Seriously?" he tilts his head to the side, his cheek flaming red.

"That was just the warning," I say before bunching my fist up and striking him upwards in the nose.

He cries out in pain, grabbing his face with both his hands, and I take the opportunity to run in the opposite direction.

Those mandatory staff self-defence classes the university made me do have finally paid off.

"Dr Cooke, get the Professor out of here!" I scream, running over to Griffin, who is fending off blows while Ciara straddles his body.

He's yelling at her to stop, but fortunately the actual punches don't seem to be hurting him. The replica shield lies on the floor a few feet beside them, almost forgotten.

I grab one of her arms and try and pull her off, but lose

my grip and falter backwards, only to slip on the shield; the pressure of my foot causes it to slide against the slick floor. Yelping, my weight goes over the side of my ankle, the pain shoots through my leg as I try and stand up. Bending my other knee for better balance, I stand like a flamingo perched on one leg, watching the two of them unsuccessfully wrestle.

Out of the corner of my eye I see Dr Cooke try and grab the Professor's arm but the Professor gives him a quick shove.

"Don't you tell me what to do!" he exclaims, picking up Dr Cooke's book. "Bloody celebrity my arse! The only thing this is good for is wiping up after the loo!"

Ciara looks up at the two men arguing and the distraction is enough to allow Griffin to throw Ciara off of him. He scrambles to his feet.

"You fight like a wuss!" she yells and lunges at him again, her red hair looking like an angry beehive on top of her head.

"Stop hitting me!" he exclaims as the two of them get into a hand slapping match. Dr Cooke comes and grabs Ciara from behind and wraps his arms around her in a tight bear hug, her legs now flailing in the air.

"Tobias!" she screams, and I turn to see him running over, wiping the blood off his face from his nosebleed.

His movements are extremely unsteady, obviously moving on pure adrenaline rather than actual strength as blood still runs freely from his nose.

Still only able to balance on my one foot I begin to shout

a warning, but out of nowhere the Professor whacks Tobias in the front of his face with the large book, causing him to crumple to the floor.

"Right, well, we've found one other use for it then," the Professor says and drops Dr Cooke's book onto the floor.

Ciara has stopped struggling now, her feet back on the floor.

"Get his car keys," I instruct Griffin, who stands beside me, looking down at Tobias.

He finds them in his pocket, then turns to evaluate Ciara.

"What about her?" Griffin asks.

I turn to Ciara who looks utterly shocked with the events.

"She's got no way of following us," I say, putting my hand on his arm. "Come on, we have to go now."

I try and take a step, but the pain in my ankle causes my knee to buckle, and I grasp onto Griffin's shoulder for support.

"What's wrong?" Griffin immediately puts his hand under my elbow to help me stand.

"She took a nasty tumble on that flying saucer," the Professor points to the fake shield that slid a few feet away during my fall. "Saw the whole thing, it was very ungraceful."

"How did you even get it?" I ask Griffin, trying to look at the replica and ensure we didn't damage it.

"How do you bloody think? I took it out of the display case, because guess what? It wasn't even locked!" He throws his arms in the air.

Dr Cooke looks at Tobias, passed out cold. "I think we should leave before the big brute wakes up."

"I'll have to carry you," Griffin says, bending over to my knees.

"No you, ahh!" I exclaim as he wraps his arms around my knees and hoists me over his shoulder. He's hoisted me way too high, and my upper thighs rest on his shoulder and I'm left awkwardly dangling down his back. "I can walk!"

"You can't even stand," he argues, trying to see my face, which just causes us both to spin. "Can I just be in charge of one thing, please?"

I roll my eyes and push up my glasses that sit very precariously on the tip of my nose.

"We'll leave you that shield," I say to Ciara, who is still staring at Tobias passed out on the floor. "He'll come to in a bit. He's just been knocked out."

Her eyes are wide and I think she's only standing up straight because of Dr Cooke's support.

"Come on, let's go," I say to Griffin, feeling at this point like I'm reining my own horse.

Griffin follows the Professor towards the door, my body bouncing on his back. Ciara walks over to Tobias and lightly shakes him with a worried look on her face.

After exiting the Exhibition Hall, Griffin turns around, causing me to spin again.

"Where's that bloody security guard?" Griffin asks, and

I can hear the judgment in his voice. "I tell you, this place is just asking for it!"

Chapter Seventeen

Once we're safely back in the car– I won't mention how I was practically *thrown* into the seat– I reach for my knapsack and take out the separate parts of my phone.

"What are you doing?" Griffin asks.

"I've got to make a call," I say, putting the sim card and battery back in.

"You can't do that!" he argues. "That's how they are tracking you."

"Tracking me? They've already found us!" I say, shaking my head at him.

"Who are you calling?" he demands. "Tell me it's not Charles."

"It's not Charles," I assure him. "It's the only person I can think of that can help us right now."

I scroll through my recent text messages: the one from Max is first on the list. I click the SEND button and the phone begins to dial his number.

Griffin puts the meter on before pulling out of the car park and I will myself to not rip the thing off the dashboard.

"June?" I hear on the other line.

"It's me," I say, putting my finger to my other ear so I can hear him better.

"What's going on? Are you all right? Where are you?" he reels off questions one after the other.

"Shouldn't you know where I am? You are still a part of the Alliance, aren't you?" I ask.

"Charles has me working separately. I haven't heard from him in a few hours."

"We're fine. We've just been to Sutton-Hoo," I respond.

"Sutton-Hoo? What were you doing there?" he asks.

I ignore his question. "Max, did you get the cameras restored?"

He pauses before he answers and my heart sinks at what that means. "June, I was able to restore the feed, but there is nothing within a ten minute window before or after the Shield was taken. It picks up your grandfather coming in, knocking over the Manuscript, and then everyone leaving the room. After that the feed is missing until we all come back in the room with Charles and by then the Shield is gone."

I close my eyes and tell myself to breathe through the panic.

"It gets worse," Max hedges. "The main stairwell that you took to leave the museum is missing its feed too, as well as the back staircase. For the *exact* same time. The cameras are hosted on a remote feed and after taking a closer look… June, someone deleted that time frame. It's gone."

I look down at my hands and see that they are shaking.

"Charles still thinks I took it?"

"I don't think he even knows what he thinks anymore." I can hear the concern in Max's voice. "He's a mess, June. He hasn't even cancelled the Gala. He still thinks he'll get the Shield back in time."

I shake my head at Charles's typical behaviour. Always assured that somehow things will work out, but maybe this time he knows something that we don't and that optimism isn't so unfounded. I can only hope.

"Max, how were you recruited into the Alliance?" I ask him suddenly.

He pauses on the phone.

"What do you mean?"

"I mean, how were you recruited?" I repeat.

"I told you, I received an email," he says.

"I remember you told me that when we met, which got me thinking. Charles doesn't really know anything about technology. He's a self-proclaimed idiot when it comes to computers, so why would he have chosen that way to contact you?"

"I don't know," Max says, puzzled. "Maybe because he knew that I was technologically inclined? I just assumed it was some sort of security measure, because it was back coded. I wasn't even able to trace the original sender."

I shake my head. "He must have had someone to help him."

"June, I'm not sure what you're getting at here," Max

says.

"Tobias isn't ex-M15, the Professor just knocked him out with a book," I say. "And I'm pretty sure Ciara is a hired actress. Charles must have known when you weren't able to trace the emails he sent you that you wouldn't be able to fix the security cameras or get the footage back."

"What? June, what are you saying?"

"I'm saying that I am not sure anymore if Charles is as innocent and frantic as he appears to be. He's hired people to look after a priceless artefact who really have no business doing so. And I think he hired me to take the fall for it."

"What?" Max asks, and I can hear the tone of disbelief in his voice. "June, that doesn't make any sense. The Alliance is one of Oxford's oldest secret societies!"

"It's all starting to make sense," I argue. "If Charles wanted to steal that Shield he couldn't just take it. He needed someone to take the fall or he would never get away with it. Anyone present when it was stolen would be a suspect, but throw me into the mix— a direct relative of the person who was already accused of stealing the Shield— and there's your scapegoat. Anyone standing next to me would look as innocent as a lamb. All he has to do is say I was protecting my grandfather, and that's why I did it."

"Okay, let's say Charles did take it. What's he going to do with it now?" Max asks.

"I don't know," I say, because honestly I don't have a clue. "Sell it, maybe? Why does anyone steal a priceless relic?

It's not like he can put it up on his mantle, is it?"

Max is silent but I can hear him breathing, obviously trying to process this whole thing.

"So, what are you going to do?" he asks me.

I look at the Professor and Dr Cooke in the back of the car. They have both dedicated their lives to history and have nothing to show for it.

"I'm not sure, but I'll let you know when I do," I say.

I hang up the phone and quickly take it apart and return it to my knapsack.

"What did he say?" Griffin asks.

"The camera footage is gone, wiped clean for the time the Shield was stolen."

Griffin nods as though he didn't expect anything else.

"Okay, so you proved the Shield is real. It still doesn't mean you stole it! What proof do they have?" Griffin voices in outrage.

"What proof do they *need*?" I shake my head. "This is old news for our family. We've never done well in the court of public opinion."

"But that's just it," Dr Cooke says, leaning forwards from the backseat. "If the Shield is real, and it came from that mound, *who* took it out? Where has it been this whole time?"

The Professor narrows his eyes at Dr Cooke.

"Albert, I'm on your side here. I've never once thought for a second that you took that Shield," Dr Cooke says, turning towards the Professor. "And my dear friend, I'm sorry I ever gave anyone else anything but that impression."

The car stays quiet, Griffin and my eyes meet as we wait for the reaction.

The Professor looks at Dr Cooke whose eyes are pleading for his forgiveness.

"I shall take it under advisement," the Professor says, pulling his notepad out from his pocket and jotting something down.

"I wish every day that we never opened that bloody tomb," Dr Cooke says, trying to peer over the Professor's shoulder to see what he is writing. "You remember we couldn't even find the crowbar that morning? We should have stopped looking while we were ahead!"

"That's it!" I say, grabbing Griffin's arm, causing him to swerve into the next lane. "That's what was wrong in those old photos! It wasn't the Shield's markings that were wrong, it was the *tomb's*."

I turn around excitedly to look at the two men in the back seat.

"You said you donated the exact tools that were used in your excavation project, right?"

"Yes," Dr Cooke nods.

"There were two markings on the wooden top plate, one with a two pronged gouge and one with a single. The tools on display were all two pronged."

"I'm not following my dear," Dr Cooke looks confused.

"Someone else opened that tomb, someone other than your team. The markings prove it!"

"You think it was plundered before we even arrived?" The Professor inquires.

"If someone had got there before you, it would have to be very shortly before— weeks at the most. The markings on the ground from the Shield were too close in measurement to the actual relic for it to be any earlier than that. The ground would have settled and the earth would have moved, especially with a group of archaeologists digging all around it," I shoot out the facts in a flurry from my excitement. "Also, your notes would have indicated that the outside of the mound had been disturbed, but there is nothing in your journal to say that it was."

"No, I don't recall any disturbances. Daniel?" The Professor asks.

Dr Cooke looks a little stunned at the Professor addressing him in such a civil manner.

"None," he adamantly denies.

"So, someone must have opened the tomb and taken the Shield right before you uncovered it," I say, reaching into my knapsack and pulling out the Professor's old journal. "Here! You even wrote that the top came off much easier than any other mound uncovered!"

I point to the part in the journal that I had only read the day before.

"The morning didn't start off well, lost the bloody crowbars if you

can believe it. *I must have put them down next to the toilets and forgot about them. We lost some daylight searching, but luckily the top came away surprisingly easily, far more than the other tombs they uncovered last week.*"

"Not surprised with the security they've got," Griffin comments.

"So, someone took the Shield, and did what with it?" Dr Cooke asks.

"I don't know, but listen to this," I say, turning to the next page in the journal. "*Daniel and I are eager to return tomorrow to study the markings some more, though I am sad to say the discovery—or lack of discovery as some see it— has discouraged some of the volunteers, and caused some of them to pack it in early. My eager pupil has even abandoned the cause when he heard of a promising new dig in Sheffield. It may not be the treasure itself, but the markings alone could prove to be of great historical significance.*"

"It was one of the volunteers?" Dr Cooke asks, clearly stunned by the revelation.

"I don't know," I shrug my shoulders. "But it's the only lead we have. If we can find out who Charles acquired the piece from to start with, then we might be able to trace who stole it originally."

"Slight problem with that," Griffin points out. "He's not very likely to open up to you about that if he's currently trying to frame you for a crime he committed, is he?"

I stay quiet, processing that as a fair point.

"Also, speaking of the crime at hand, it doesn't really

help much to know who nicked it in the first place if it still means everyone thinks you've stolen it *now*."

All valid points.

"Well we can't just sit around and do *nothing*," I argue.

"Unless," the Professor raises his index finger, "we can prove that your friend bought the piece from the original thief."

"It doesn't prove that June didn't steal the Shield from the museum, though," Griffin points out.

"Of course it doesn't, but it does cast doubt on whether she *did*," the Professor comments.

"Is that enough? Doubt?" Griffin asks.

"My boy, you are a playwright, are you not?" the Professor asks. "There is only one thing the public love more than scandal. It's when people get their comeuppance."

Chapter Eighteen

I manage to hobble back into Ruth's house with just the aid of Griffin's arm around my waist. After Ruth puts something that smells like week old garbage and hurts like the Dickens on my ankle, she sends me off to bed and tells me not to move until the morning.

I don't sleep a wink, and I'm under no illusion that it's because of the pain in my ankle. I can hear Griffin's pacing steps above me and know he isn't getting any sleep either.

The Shield is real. After all these years I never would have believed it was possible.

It seems crazy, but now that the Shield is actually real and there is some credible proof that the tomb was opened before the Professor's team was there, strangely enough I feel a glimmer of hope.

It's bizarre, I know. Everything is going to pot, and really I'm not sure if Charles will ever admit to me who he acquired it from. But it's something. It's a little seed of hope that has been planted.

I feel beyond guilty for all this time never believing my grandfather. Of course, I believed he didn't steal it, but I never looked beyond the surface of what his mind was so adamantly trying to tell me. I think he knew the Shield was real from the very start. By going down into that tomb alone, I think the existence of the Shield was planted in his brain and he was never able to shake it. With the disease he slowly started to lose those filters that we all have, those filters that allow us to keep quiet and not voice the absurd thoughts we think every day. But his thoughts were real, and I wonder if the reason he has held on so tightly to his innocence all these years, to drench himself in the scandal over and over again with newspaper clippings and his journals, was his mind's way of not letting him forget that the Shield was out there. A part of history was out there somewhere, and he didn't want to forget that.

As I sit at the breakfast table the next morning I'm able to fully rotate my ankle again thanks to Ruth's special ointment, though it's still sore.

"I told you," Ruth says, placing toast down in front of me. "One rub of my Mum's special remedy and you're as good as rain again."

I smile at her but don't quite meet her eyes. She went shopping for me, like she somehow expected we would be back here. She knew my size– my *exact* size. She also bought me new undergarments, which were sitting on the edge of my bed when I woke up. I'm not sure where she put my other clothes.

I've never had a woman figure in my life to do those things for me. The Professor used to order all my clothes from a catalogue when I was younger, always a size or two too big so I had room to grow. It's just a little unnerving, that's all.

"Productive evening?" she asks, taking us all in around the table.

No one has spoken much this morning, all lost in thought, I suppose. Now that I know the Shield is real and that we are being set up, the problem just seems to have gotten bigger. I suppose I tackled the less complicated problem first: if the Shield was just a well-produced replica it would have been a domino effect and we would have been in the clear— surely no one would be this concerned over a replica.

But now that I am positive the Shield is authentic, it raises too many questions for my mind to handle at once. Who stole the Shield all those years ago and how did it end up at the Ashmolean? Did Charles create the Alliance for the sole purpose of leading me to the Shield in order to frame me?

I look to Griffin then dart my eyes to his Mum, indicating that we can't talk in front of her.

"Er— Mum, you know I was telling the Professor only yesterday about your lovely lemon cookies. You don't think you could whip us up a batch, do you?"

"No lemons, love," Ruth says apologetically.

"No lemons?" the Professor says, as a distant look comes in his eyes. "I have a lemon bush in the garden. June

Bug, you know where our lemons are."

My eyes widen, I look from the Professor to Ruth, briefly shaking my head. We never had any lemon tree.

He was doing so well. Last night, after everything that happened, I was sure he would slip away on the car ride home, but he was even a little engaging with Dr Cooke towards the end of the journey.

"I will get you the lemons, Ruth," the Professor says, pushing back his chair, ready to stand, clearly getting agitated.

Ruth quickly stands up and puts out a reassuring hand to the Professor. "No need Albert, I was just popping out to the shops anyways. I'll get the lemons."

She starts to collect the plates and the Professor also stands up. "I'll come along. We're out of whiskey again. House is drier than a bloody desert."

Ruth puts the plates down, and quickly makes her way to the door. "It's alright, Albert, I'll only be a minute."

I've never seen someone move that quickly before in my life. She takes a bright purple-checkered scarf off of the coat tree and slips on her wellies. She ties the scarf over her head, covering the curlers before turning and waving goodbye.

She's actually gone out in them. And her quilted dressing gown.

I look toward Griffin who doesn't seem to think it's strange in the slightest.

The Professor leisurely takes his seat again before picking up his cup of tea.

"You were going to say, June?" he asks before taking a sip.

I narrow my eyes at him.

"How often do you do that?" I say.

He raises his eyebrows at me. "I'm not sure I know what you are referring to."

"I'm referring to the fact that you seem to be able to turn your "forgetful moments" on and off like a lamp," I say, crossing my arms.

"The mind is a tricky thing, I'm afraid," he says, shrugging and turning to Dr Cooke. "Comes and goes without a moment's notice."

Dr Cooke tries to hide his smile behind his own teacup.

"Look, the important thing is Mum is gone," Griffin says, though even he seems to be amused by the whole thing. "What is the plan of action, June?"

I take a deep breath, ready to receive the outrage.

"I need to go to the Gala tonight," I say.

Everyone is quiet except Griffin who sighs. "I think you're right."

I look up in shock. "You think I'm *right?*"

"Well, the Professor himself said that without any solid proof all we have to go on is doubt. We have to get Charles to admit he bought the piece, and I don't see any other way you're going to be able to speak with him. He'll never expect you to go to the Gala, so it might catch him off guard," Griffin explains. "Would a guilty person really show up to the scene of the crime?"

"Can't believe the git is still putting the whole thing on, to be honest," Dr Cooke says. "What is he going to say when the guests show up?"

"He might just be planning to show the other artefacts from Sutton-Hoo," I say. "It's not often they are out of London."

"June, you'll have to iron out my suit," the Professor says decisively.

"You are not coming," I argue.

"I bloody well am!" he says. "It's not only your name that needs to be cleared tonight."

"I'm coming too then," Dr Cooke nods decisively. "Do you think tweed would be alright?"

"I think my dad had a few extra suits that my Mum put in the attic," Griffin says, getting up from the table. "I hope Mum ironed my dress shirt."

"You're coming too?" I ask him.

"I've got to see the final act," he says, as if any other option is ludicrous.

I look around as the men bustle about tidying up the dishes, the excitement in the air palpable. Which is all well and good, but it's because they think it is all going to work out.

"What am I going to wear?" I say, looking down at the jumper Ruth bought me.

"I'll ring Mum, she'll pick you something up while she's

at the shops," Griffin says, carrying the plates into the kitchen.

"I think we are forgetting just one problem here," I say, trying to get them to slow down and think this thing through. "How are we even going to get in? It's invitation only."

Griffin nods his head. "You best get on the phone then and get us four invitations."

Chapter Nineteen

I climb the narrow ladder leading to the attic, trying to balance the tray of tea and biscuits with one hand while the other steadies me. My ankle is still a bit precarious from the night before, but I can walk on it which is a good sign.

I hear banging from above, a hammer hitting something metal.

"I'm doing it Mum!" Griffin yells.

When he sees my head pop through the hole in the floor he immediately puts the hammer down and picks up the magazine he was obviously just reading.

"Oh good, I thought you were Mum," he says, pointing to my head, which is full of curlers.

If I had any free hands I would start to pull every single last one out.

"Your Mum is giving me a makeover," I try not to sound like it is the last thing on this earth that I want done to me.

She came at me with the curlers— she keeps a spare set in the bathroom— and they are so tightly wrapped around my hair I think it might look as though I've just had a facelift. She tried to have a go at tweezing my eyebrows but I decided there needed to be a line drawn somewhere, and very quickly.

"What are you working on?" I say, putting the tray down. I look around and find an empty bucket in the corner, which I flip over and settle myself on top of.

"Mum wants me to fix the window," he points to the small circular window on the wall that has duct tape all around the edges. "She says it lets in a draft."

"Right," I say, nodding and looking around the room.

It's full of junk. Piles and piles of paper everywhere, an artificial Christmas tree in the corner that's missing it's top half and dozens of boxes labelled 'clothes'.

"What are these?" I say, reaching behind me to pick up one of the piles of paper

"Some of my plays," he answers before looking back down at the magazine in his hand.

"Oh wow, you've written so many!" I say, taking in the large stacks of them scattered around me.

I open the first bound one in my hand and start to read some of it. It's actually pretty funny. A little dark, but pretty funny. Flipping through to the end I see that it just stops midsentence. Taking the next one in the pile I begin flipping through it as well, but the end is also missing.

"They're not finished," I say, looking through the pile on my knee.

"Nope," he agrees, not looking up.

"But, why don't you finish them?" I ask, looking around. "There have to be dozens here."

"I get a new idea and then start on that instead," he shrugs.

I look around the room again and realise that some of these have to be a decade old from the way the paper has coloured.

"You don't plan on finishing any of them?" I ask.

"Maybe one day," he says, putting his magazine down and looking at the pile in my hand. "I don't know how any of them end yet."

"Have you finished any?" I ask.

"Not yet," Griffin sighs, taking in all of his work around the room. "Endings are the trickiest part."

"I've heard it's the middle," I say, putting the stack of papers back down where I got them.

"That's what everyone thinks," he says, waving off my observation. "It doesn't matter if your beginning and middle are brilliant, if the ending is garbage it's all anyone will remember."

"So how come you can't come up with any endings?" I ask him.

"Well, when does something really ever end? When do you know it's done? Really our stories don't end until we're dead and even then life still goes on, doesn't it?" he asks in wonderment.

"I suppose you could just end the story when things are good," I suggest. "I always like a happy ending."

"Happy endings are out now," Griffin says as though

everyone should know that.

"End when it's gone to shit, then," I counter.

"Too gloomy, you've got to give them some hope at least," he argues.

"You're never going to finish these, are you?" I ask.

He gets up and walks over to the window, lifting up a piece of the duct tape that has fallen down. He sticks it back to the window frame, but seconds later it drops down again, the stickiness of the tape clearly gone.

"Why are you helping me?" I ask him, standing up as well. "If you don't have any of these done to give to a producer, why do you even care if you are caught up in this?"

He looks up at me, studying my face with a frown. I wonder if he's even stopped to think about what he's doing in the last few days or if he just got caught up in the excitement of it all.

"How did it end for Raedwald?" he asks. "After his son died, what happened?"

I'm not really sure how that answers my question.

"Not a lot really," I say, shrugging. "After the battle where his son died it's really Edwin, the exiled nobleman, who comes into the limelight."

"See, that's just what I mean!" Griffin argues. "Do you finish the story at the Shield? Surely there has to be more to Raedwald's life than just that."

"Well, that's not to say he did *nothing*," I explain. "When the Battle of the River Idle was won, King Raedwald appointed Edwin King of the Anglia, and Edwin remained under Raedwald's thumb until Raedwald's death."

"So what happened to this Edwin?"

"Actually, he has his own intrigue. When his daughter was first born in 626 the West Saxons were upset with how he had gained his title of King. They sent a messenger to kill him with a poisoned dagger but his minister stepped in front of the blade and was killed instead. It is believed that Christianity was then reinstated because of the minister's sacrifice."

"I'd already be on the second play," Griffin admits.

We sit in silence, looking around at the mess, before Griffin stands up.

"Where are the others? Shouldn't we be going soon?"

"We don't have to leave for a few hours yet," I say, looking at my watch. "Max said not to show up before six-thirty."

"Are you sure we can trust him?" Griffin asks, crossing his arms across his chest.

"He's been helping us so far," I argue, though really I'm not sure I can really trust anyone right now. "He told me to get out of the house, to take my phone apart. I don't think he would tell me those things if he wanted us to get caught."

"Why is he helping you?"

"I think he feels like we are sort of the same," I try and explain from the little I know about him. "His grandfather loved Ancient History; Max said he used to admire the

Professor's work. I think it might have just been him and his grandfather growing up as well, just like me and the Professor."

"So he's willing to go to jail because you were both only children?" Griffin asks, and I can hear the tone of disbelief.

"You're doing it to get in the papers," I hotly point out. "What does it even matter why he is doing it as long as it helps me?"

"It's just strange, you only just met," Griffin says, oblivious to the fact that I could argue the same thing to him. "I just think he has to be after something."

"After what?" I frown in confusion, unsure as to what he's getting at.

Griffin widens his eyes and looks me up and down, insinuating exactly what he thinks Max is after.

"Oh grow up!" I argue, rolling my eyes. "Maybe he just knows what it's like to live your whole life for someone else. He told me his grandfather wasn't well towards the end."

"Alright, he's a saint," Griffin says, deciding he doesn't want to talk about Max anymore. "Where are the Professor and Dr Cooke?"

"In the garden. Dr Cooke is trying to keep him away from your mother in case he has one of his 'episodes'," I answer, thinking back to earlier. "To be honest, it's nice to have someone else to keep him company for a bit."

"I'm sure it's a lot of work," Griffin says.

"I've only really lived with him for the past ten years," I

say, looking at the window and down into the garden. "I grew up in boarding schools, so I only saw him on the holidays. He was always so busy; he didn't really have time to raise a little girl. Probably didn't have the first clue how either."

"I used to pray my Mum would send me to boarding school," Griffin says. "Especially when I was a teenager. She has a tendency to smother a little."

I touch the curlers in my hair and decide not to make a comment.

"Well, all I wanted to do was get out of boarding school. The other girls were more interested in the boys' school across the village, and all I was interested in was history," I smile.

"So you were *that* kid," Griffin says.

"The Professor told me I wasn't allowed to stay at home with him because he was always away on his next adventure. He was called to dig sites for weeks or months on end, and it wasn't the right place to bring a little girl," I explain. "So I learnt all about the history he loved so much, hoping that if I knew enough, he might take me along with him one day. In the end, I loved it just as much as he did."

"I bet you wished you were back at school when you finally got to live with him," Griffin guesses.

"I was only home for about a month before I noticed that something was wrong. It took me a few months after that to convince him to take the medication the doctor had suggested. It's more the mental strain than anything else," I admit. "To listen to the same things, over and over again. Hearing him repeat his innocence, his defence– even though I believed him, he looked at me as though I was judging him. Though now I know he was right; I realise I should have stood up for him more."

"June, you did what you could," Griffin argues.

"I used to get so upset," I say. "Rolling my eyes, muttering behind his back. He used to ramble over and over again about his innocence– even when no one was talking to him about it he would purposely bring it up in the conversation. He's got a million different theories as to what happened, each more absurd than the next and– Oh God!"

"What?" Griffin asks.

"That's what I'm doing!" I say, covering my hand with my mouth. "I keep repeating myself, over and over again."

"Okay?" Griffin frowns.

"You know how woman always worry that they are turning into their mothers?" I ask, the fear clear on my face. "It's happened. I'm turning into him!"

"Okay, calm down," Griffin obviously sees I am about to get hysterical.

"I can't! You heard me at Dr Cooke's house, at Sutton-Hoo. Tobias keeps rolling his eyes at *me!* I always roll my eyes at him," I say, pointing out the window in the direction of the Professor and Dr Cooke, who sits on the bench at the end of the garden.

"I think it's the pain talking, from your ankle. You shouldn't be standing on it like this. We'll go downstairs and get you some more medicine." Griffin says, more reassuring himself than me.

"That's what I always tell him!" I say, looking out the window and wondering what I've become.

Chapter Twenty

I tug on the hem of the dress, willing it to cover more of my upper thigh, but it only causes the neckline to plunge even lower.

"You look lovely," Ruth says, clasping her hands together as she stands on the edge of the driveway.

I look like a prostitute.

It didn't look so bad when she took it out of the bag– I mean, it's a black dress: how can you really go wrong? But after putting it on I realised the dress is a real life optical illusion: when it's off there seems to be loads of fabric, but when you put it on the material mysteriously disappears somewhere into the unknown.

"And look at that hair," she says, tousling the soft curls surrounding my face.

Begrudgingly I have to admit that the curls are a vast improvement to the strands that normally sit flat against my face.

"Griffin, doesn't your lady friend look nice?"

"Beautiful," Griffin nods, but he doesn't even look at me before he kisses his Mum on her cheek. "Don't wait up."

Griffin actually looks pretty smart in his black suit with

his hair gelled back. The white scarf around his neck gives an artistic touch to his suit.

"You didn't even look!" His mother smacks him lightly on the arm. "Considering all the time we had to spend to get her looking like this, the least you could do is admire her properly."

I strain to see the compliment in there somewhere amidst the insult.

Griffin rolls his eyes at his Mum before looking at me. His eyes widen as he takes in my appearance, and I quickly try and tug down the hem of my skirt again.

"You do look nice," he says it as though it's not something he expected.

"Thank you," I say, trying not to let the bitterness through in my voice.

"She shouldn't wear her glasses," Ruth mutters, even though I explicitly told her I couldn't see my own two feet without them.

"No, she should keep them," Griffin says while still looking at me. "They suit her."

Not wishing to be under the pair's inspection any longer, I look past Griffin to see the Professor and Dr Cooke leaving the house.

"A *white* suit?" I ask, flabbergasted as the Professor strolls by Ruth towards the car.

"Smashing, isn't it?" the Professor says, tipping the matching top hat in my direction.

"It was Griffin's father's wedding suit," Ruth looks at it fondly.

"I wanted that one," Dr Cooke mumbles as he walks past wearing a brown suit made of a shiny, reflective material that looks right out of a scene from Saturday Night Fever.

"Well, I got it first," the Professor says, running his hand over the rim of the top hat. "Besides, it never would have fit. You're wearing an elastic band to button your trousers up as it is."

"You realise we are supposed to try and be inconspicuous?" I look at the pair of them and I have to giggle at how ridiculous they look.

"Oh, the whole thing will be full of a bunch of eccentric academics," the Professor waves away my concern. "We'll fit right in."

"Right, we better get on with it," Griffin says, looking at his wristwatch. "What time are we supposed to be there for?"

"Max will meet us at the back door at seven," I repeat for the tenth time in the last hour.

"It's a shame you don't have an extra ticket," Ruth pouts, wrapping her arms around her quilted dressing gown. "I would have liked to go for a bit of fun."

My eyes can't help but drift up to the curlers in her hair.

She still has no clue what is going on, even though she's been pressing me for details all afternoon. Dr Cooke kept the Professor in the garden most of the day in case he started rambling about the Shield.

"I've had the tickets for weeks I'm afraid, Ruth," I apologise again. "Forgot all about it until the Professor reminded me this morning."

"Next time," Griffin promises her before walking to the car and getting in the driver's side.

I offer her a wave and get in the car after helping the Professor with his door.

"Everyone know what their job is?" I ask, though I've repeated it enough times today that if they don't know it by now I think it's safe to say they'll never get it.

"Wrote mine down in here somewhere," the Professor says, pulling his notebook from his pocket.

"Did you also write down in there that you forgave me?" Dr Cooke asks, peering over his shoulder. "I think you might have forgotten to do that last night."

"All I see is a note here saying you admitted how wrong you were," the Professor says, flipping his notebook shut. "And something about half of your royalties."

"I said no such thing—"

Griffin raises his eyes to the ceiling before sighing.

"Max is meeting us all at the back door at seven, at which point Dr Cooke and I will enter the main atrium and start mingling with the guests. Hopefully we'll get the attention of Beavis and Butthead," Griffin recites.

"Right," I say, choosing not to remind him again to not underestimate Tobias and Ciara. "The Professor and I will go up to the Special Events room. It's set to open at eight o'clock, but Max said Charles is going at seven-thirty to make sure everything is finalised for the setup; hopefully if you two keep Tobias and Ciara occupied he will be alone."

"It seems simple enough," Griffin shrugs.

"That's just getting in," I remind him. "I still have to figure out how to convince Charles to tell me who he acquired the Shield from when he could very well be the very person who stole it."

"So, how are you going to do that, then?" Griffin asks, turning the ignition and putting the car into drive.

"Not a clue," I say, shaking my head. "You didn't put the meter on."

I point to the dashboard, where the taxi's meter is currently shut off.

Griffin hesitates for a moment.

"Don't you need that as proof of your alibi?" I point out.

"You didn't steal that Shield, June," Griffin says, briefly turning his face to look at me. "That's all I'll be saying to the courts."

I turn my face to look at the road in front of us, willing my eyes to stay dry as a smile spreads over my lips.

Chapter Twenty-One

"Quickly!" Max waves us over as he holds one of the service entrance doors to the museum open. "I've only managed to block out the camera to this stairwell for three minutes. I've told the security team I need to manually reset one of the cameras because of a glitch in the feed."

We parked a few blocks away at the Red Lion Square and ran most of the way to the Ashmolean, constantly checking over our shoulders to see if we were followed.

"June, you look..." Max stands up straight and takes me in from head to toe, a slight blush on his forehead. "Nice dress."

I offer him a hurried smile as I pass him in the narrow corridor.

Once we are all inside, Max squeezes past us to open another doorway. "The guests are on the next floor," he says, pointing up. "Three floors above that is the Special Events room. This door leads right to the outside of the room where the artefacts are being kept."

I nod, looking at him. "What about you? Where are you going to be?"

"I have to go back to the security room. They'll know

something is up if I don't," he explains. "I'll keep an eye on you, though. If there is any problem, or any change to the schedule, I will send a message to your phone. You did bring it, right?"

Max takes a look again at my dress, obviously contemplating where a mobile phone could possibly be hidden.

Griffin takes a step forward to block his view.

"She has it," he offers Max a smile.

"Better get a move on, June Bug," the Professor says, tipping his hat to Max as he starts to climb the stairs.

"Max, thank you," I shake my head, not knowing what to say. "I promise that if this doesn't work out they'll never know it was you that helped me—"

"You're innocent, June, you and I both know it," Max says, not a single trace of doubt in his voice. "I hope you get whatever you need to prove it."

I offer him another smile before Griffin takes my hand and pulls me to the staircase.

"We've got to go," he says to Max, and I lift my hand to wave before I turn and start climbing the stairs.

We find the Professor and Dr Cooke waiting on the first floor stairwell, the Professor adjusting his bow tie.

"Right," Griffin says, nodding to the door before looking back at me. "This is it, then."

I nod back, the sweat starting to collect in my palms at the thought of what we are about to do.

"It's going to be okay," Griffin places his hand on my arm.

"I know," I reply, though I think we are both just saying what we think we are supposed to.

"You asked me in the attic why I'm doing this," he says. "I'm doing this for you."

He looks at me, and I can feel him almost willing everything to work out before kissing my cheek.

Turning to Dr Cooke, Griffin nods.

"It's showtime," Griffin says, and opens the side door that leads to the atrium.

The door is only open for a minute, but there doesn't seem to be anyone directly outside of it. I can hear the guests' voices carrying through the hallway.

Looking at the Professor, we both push our glasses further up our noses before climbing the rest of the stairs. At the top I pull the door open, inch-by-inch, trying to peer into the hallway to make sure the coast is clear. I pull the door the rest of the way open and wave the Professor into the hall.

Griffin is right. The lack of security for priceless artefacts really is atrocious. I mean, I know there are guards in the atrium not allowing people up, but it really wouldn't be that hard to get around them.

I walk as quietly as possible across the tiled floor, the Professor following right behind me. I look up at the security camera pointing down directly outside the side door of the

Special Events room and pray that Max was able to block that camera as well. Testing the door handle, it turns smoothly and I smile at the reaction Griffin would have if he were here.

Walking into the well-lit room seems almost surreal. It feels like a lifetime ago when I walked in here last, but it was only a few days ago. I close the door carefully behind the Professor but I spin around when I hear him cry out.

"What in the blazes is going on here?" he exclaims.

I turn around and have to grab onto the wall.

There, in the centre display case, is the Shield of Quell.

"It's– what–" I stumble to make a coherent sentence. "It's back!"

We both slowly approach the display case, cautious, as though it might somehow attack us. As we both circle the piece, looking at it from every angle available, the frown on my forehead just gets deeper.

"Is it a replica?" I ask the Professor. "Did they create a duplicate to display for the Gala?"

He shakes his head. "It looks just as real as the one I saw a few days ago," he argues.

I look at the leather, the tarnished edges a perfect match to the shield I studied just a few days before.

"But– How did it get back here? Who stole it and why would they *return* it?" I ask, bewildered.

"I don't know," the Professor says, leaning forward to look more closely at the detailing on the boss. "But I don't bloody like it one bit."

Now that I have seen the markings more clearly at the exhibit, I study the unique boss, each gemstone a different depth from the one beside it. It truly is a remarkable piece.

We hear noise from the hall; the sound of voices are on the other side of the door and my eyes dart around, realising there is nowhere to hide.

Charles opens the main door to the room, his back turned to us as he addresses the few men standing behind him.

"More spectacular than you could ever imagine," he says with a flourish, before turning and stopping dead in his tracks when he sees the Professor and I standing next to the Shield.

"June?" Charles sputters.

The Professor and I don't move, unsure where to go or what to say. We stand like statues and watch Charles's bewildered face.

"What the fu–" Realising the men are still standing behind him, watching the scene, Charles quickly changes tactics. "Er– sorry, I didn't realise you were in here. I thought you weren't coming by until later."

His eyes are wide and the smile on his face twitches slightly.

As he darts his eyes to the men behind him I realise he wants me to play along with his act for their sake. Realising someone would call security and I won't be able to get anything out of him if I start hurling accusations in front of them, I decide to go along with it.

"I– er– was just checking the Shield," I say, my mind finally making a coherent thought.

"Good, good," he says, nodding his head quickly, his eyes continuously darting to the Professor, obviously expecting him to do something

"Wanted to make sure no one had run off with it before the big night," I joke, which receives laughs from the other men and causes Charles's smile to finally falter.

"Gentlemen, would you just give us a minute," Charles says, turning to them apologetically. "I just need a few words with our historical experts here before the grand unveiling."

The men look slightly confused, obviously unsure why they were asked to come to the room only to be told to go back downstairs, but they nod their agreement and leave before Charles shuts and locks the door.

"What the hell are you doing here?" he hisses, ice in his voice.

"What am *I* doing here?" I ask, raising my voice. "What is *this* doing here?"

I point past the Professor to the Shield.

"Oh come off it," Charles says, exasperation clear in his voice. "You know full well what it's doing here. And I really can't believe you would come here, tonight of all nights, with the little innocent act."

I look at him as though he's lost his marbles.

"What innocent act? What are you talking about?" I ask

him.

"I don't know what you are playing at, but you need to leave here before anyone else sees you!" Charles says, taking me by the arm.

"I don't think so. Not this time. I'm not going anywhere," I argue, pulling my elbow out of his grasp. "I'm not running anymore! I haven't done anything wrong and you know it."

Charles lets out an amused laugh before shaking his head. "What I know is that you stole the Shield a few days ago, had me running all over England trying to get it back, only to have you return it to my house this morning."

I put my hands on my hips.

"Charles I haven't taken anything, and if I had I certainly wouldn't return it to your house– how thick do you think I am?" I yell.

"Listen, I don't know why you returned it. Maybe you saw it, panicked, and just took it. Quite frankly I don't care. I tried to cover for you, but this has gone too far," Charles spits out. "This is the greatest achievement of my life and I'm not going to let you ruin it!"

"Are you even listening to yourself?" I argue. "I did not take the Shield, which means someone else did. Someone who stole it and then returned it back to you!"

"Not the bloody brightest thief, I'd say," the Professor chimes in. "Don't much see the point to be honest."

"This whole thing hasn't made any sense from the

beginning and I've finally figured out why. It's you, Charles," I say, pointing at him.

"What are you talking about?" his eyes dart from me to the Professor.

"You bought the Shield and donated it to the Ashmolean. You said it yourself, you will be curator when you've finished tonight, something you would have never achieved otherwise," I explain. "You made up some secret Alliance as a lure to get me involved because you knew I would never set foot near that thing otherwise."

"I made up the Alliance?" Charles says, raising his right eyebrow.

"Yes. I know Tobias and Ciara aren't who you say they are," I reveal. "You were going to frame me this whole time, weren't you? You donated the piece to the museum to secure the position, but what? Did you end up needing the money for the Shield more than you needed the promotion?"

"This is preposterous," he argues, but I can tell by the way he keeps touching his forehead that he is agitated.

"Is it? Or is it pretty close to the truth?" I guess. "I'm guessing the Ashmolean didn't take the loss of the Shield quite as well as you had hoped, considering it is back here tonight. You know, not everyone is as lacksey-daisy as you are about missing things, Charles."

"This is ridiculous," he says, taking a step backwards. "I'm not listening to another word."

"You were going to send me to jail for the rest of my

life!" I yell, shaking my head. "You were supposed to be my *friend*!"

The side door opens again, and we all turn just as Griffin's body is shoved through the doorway, the back of his suit jacket in Tobias's clenched fist.

"Security said you were up here," Tobias says to Charles, noting the Professor and I standing next to the Shield. "They must have come through the side entrance; their car is a few blocks away. Found these two lurking downstairs with the guests."

"I can assure you I do not *lurk*," Dr Cooke says, straightening his jacket, Ciara following closely behind him.

"She bloody kicked me, broke skin!" Griffin yells, limping as he walks forward and points at Ciara.

"You need to get them all out of here," Charles orders Tobias, looking at his watch. "The doors will be opening in five minutes."

"I'm not going anywhere!" I say, looking Charles right in the eye. "I have nothing to hide! Open the doors, let the people outside decide who the thief is."

Charles jaw clenches as his gaze moves to Tobias.

"He's in on it, isn't he?" I ask Charles, turning to Tobias and Ciara. "You're both in on this!"

Neither of them moves.

"It all makes sense. You three were the last people in this room before the Professor and I left that night. You've been planning this from the beginning. The Alliance isn't real because you aren't real!"

Ciara frowns.

"I mean, I know you're *real*. What I mean is, you are not who you say you are, and I can prove it."

I really hope they don't call my bluff right now. I look up at the camera, which is pointing down on us, and hope that Max is watching from the security room. I worry that he didn't tell me that Charles was coming up early; my phone didn't ring once. If they somehow found out he was helping me this whole time...

I just hope he managed to get out somehow.

"We couldn't understand why you wouldn't cancel the Gala when the Shield was missing. But coming after me, that was all just a show for the others, for the museum curators. You were setting me up. You didn't cancel the Gala because you had the Shield this whole time, and you knew it was going to come back."

"Get her out of here," Charles says from behind me.

"It's time to leave," Tobias orders, still holding onto Griffin's jacket.

"Oh really?" I say, tilting my head. "And how exactly do you plan on making us leave?"

Tobias offers me a hint of a smile before reaching in the back of his trousers to bring out a gun and pointing it at me. "Will this do?"

"Certainly does it for me," the Professor says, moving past us into the hallway outside.

Chapter Twenty-Two

"They can't keep us in here forever," Griffin yells, kicking the wall.

I roll my eyes at the theatrics. He's honestly done the same thing for the last few hours. At least, I think it's only been a few hours. It's hard to say at this point.

The Professor and Dr Cooke nodded off while I watched Griffin pace. Slowly the rhythmic pattern of his footsteps caused my own eyes to shut, only to be woken shortly after by another one of his rants.

Tobias and Ciara led us down the side staircase where we entered the Ashmolean and through to the other side of the building. Once there, they put us in a small utility room and locked the door. With no lock on the inside and the door clearly a steel one, nothing that Griffin has thrown at it has made the slightest difference.

"When do you think they are coming back?" he asks us again. He receives no replies.

"Well, they have to let us out sometime!" Griffin says, clearly frustrated that he is the only one who isn't taking this very calmly.

"They do have to let us out sometime, right?" Griffin

asks, the disturbing thought just entering his head. "I mean, you don't think they will just leave us here?"

"Surely not," Dr Cooke shakes his head. "Today is Sunday, possibly Monday morning now. I would think they would have to come and get us before a custodian comes and finds us."

"And then what?" Griffin asks, the panic clearly getting to him. "What are they going to do with us then?"

Dr Cooke shrugs, looking thoroughly bored with the topic after hours and hours of debate. "It's hard to say with the git running the show. Probably do us in, I should think."

"Charles may be a lot of things, but he isn't a murderer," I argue.

"Are you *seriously* still trying to defend him? After all of this?" Griffin throws his arms in the air.

"I wish I was bloody dead with all this racket!" the Professor says from the corner, his top hat tipped across his face to shield out the light from the single bulb hanging from the ceiling.

"You had to be a part of a secret Alliance," Griffin mutters under his breath, but I manage to catch the words.

"Excuse me?" I say, standing with my hands on my hips. "You really think all of this is *my* fault?"

"Whose fault would it be?" Griffin asks. "If you hadn't wanted to be a part of some stupid Alliance none of this would even be happening right now!"

"Well, I'm sorry for wanting something more for my life

227

than stares and whispers behind my back!" I yell in outrage. "I'm sorry I wanted to do something that was just for me, just once in my life."

"So take up yoga!" Griffin grabs his hair in frustration.

"You don't get it, do you? I *love* history, it's in my blood!" I exclaim. "I'm a history professor who has never been on an excavation, never had any practical study of any major discoveries in the last fifteen years because I was too afraid of something going wrong, something going missing or a site being compromised, and I would be the first one they turned on."

I look at my grandfather, who watches me and the tears that flow down my cheeks. "I know it was the hardest thing you ever had to go through in your life, but it was for me too."

He nods, his own eyes glistening with tears before he looks down to the floor. Dr Cooke puts his hand on the Professor's knee, and even though I am in a closet full of people who have put themselves in danger for me over and over again, I've never felt more alone.

"I'm sorry that it turned out this way," I say, shaking my head at Griffin. "But I'm not sorry for finally deciding to do something with my life."

I collapse back down onto a bucket and study my fingers, which are tightly clasped together.

"Charles won't hurt us," I try and reassure them.

"You think he is just going to let us go?" Griffin asks,

sceptically. "Why would he do that? He knows the first thing you would do is run to the papers."

"That's just it, I've given it a lot of thought and I think that is *exactly* what Charles would do," I say, shaking my head. "It's our word against his and we have absolutely no proof. He could even deny that the Shield was stolen in the first place!" I look over to the Professor sitting in the corner. "I think he is banking on the fact that if I say absolutely nothing, it all goes away."

"It hardly goes away!" Griffin says to me, obviously annoyed at how calmly I seem to be taking this. "You don't think people are going to start wondering where the Shield was for twenty years? You really think the Professor can live through that again?"

I straighten my back at his words. "You are acting as though I *like* this. That I don't know exactly what it is going to do to the Professor and our family. I've lived through it my whole life!" I yell at him. "If I start shouting from the rooftops about some conspiracy I have absolutely no proof of, they're going to chalk me up to being just as crazy as him."

I stand there, breathing deeply, telling myself to calm down.

"Do you honestly think we would all just stand by and not stick up for you? You're not a saint, June. You're a good person who stood up for what she thought was right. Maybe it's time you give us the courtesy to do the same thing," Griffin says. "Your grandfather was right. He's not the crazy one here."

I clench my jaw, my eyes smarting with tears as my eyes move to the Professor sitting in the corner, idly watching the two of us.

"Don't let them lead you down the rabbit hole, June Bug," he says, before closing his eyes again.

The sound of the lock in the door causes me to turn and shield my eyes as the bright natural light from the hallway invades our dark cupboard.

"It's time to go," Tobias says, one hand on the door, another on his hip.

"What? No gun this time?" Griffin asks.

"It was a fake," Tobias grins. "Found it in your car when I was doing my surveillance."

I slowly turn to look at Griffin. He looks pretty upset with himself.

"Wasn't pleasant being in that small cupboard all night, was it?" Ciara says, her arms crossed over her chest before nodding at Griffin. "I hope your leg is feeling a bit better."

Griffin grumbles and I see him purposely limp when he takes a step.

"You know we could have suffocated," he says to Ciara.

"At least we came back!" she argues. "We had to break down the wall into the bleedin' kitchen to get out of that cupboard!"

"Oh, bloody fantastic!" Dr Cooke exclaims.

"Where are you taking us?" Griffin asks the two of them.

"To your car," Tobias explains, opening the door wide.

"And then where?" I ask.

He shrugs. "Wherever you drive yourselves, I guess."

I narrow my eyes at him. "So that's it? You're just going to let us go, after all of that?"

I guess I do know Charles pretty well.

"Charles said to keep you occupied until the Gala finished," Tobias explains. "It was Ciara's idea to keep you in the cupboard until this morning."

Ciara looks at me without a trace of regret on her face. "Bit cramped I bet?"

"Listen, I don't know what Charles has offered you two—"

Tobias raises his hand to stop me. "We are not interested in hearing any more of your theories. Our job is to keep you as far away from the Shield as possible while it is here at the Ashmolean, and that is exactly what we plan to do."

"I don't want to get near the Shield!" I argue.

"Makes our jobs a lot easier then, won't it?" Ciara says to Tobias.

"What *job*? There is no Alliance," I say, shaking my head. "I thought we all came to an agreement on that last night."

"I've heard enough," Tobias says, opening the door as wide as it will go. "We are going to escort you to your car and then I don't want to see your face again."

"You can't be serious! You're just going to let us go and

hope we don't say anything to anyone?"

"You're the one that committed the crime, so I guess that's up to you and your feelings on a jail cell," Tobias shrugs. "The Alliance has talked the Ashmolean out of pressing charges, but if you push it…"

I study Tobias's serious face and realise that the innocence I see on his features isn't an act at all.

"You didn't help Charles steal the Shield, did you?" I ask.

"No." Tobias shakes his head. "Because he didn't steal the Shield. The Alliance was formed to *protect* it."

"You actually believe there is an Alliance," I state in wonderment, then look over at Griffin, who looks thoroughly confused by the whole conversation.

"Would a secret Alliance allow a priceless artefact to be stolen right out from under their noses, returned, and then let the people that supposedly stole it in the first place go scot free?" I ask them.

"Charles has informed us the Alliance will not be pressing charges for discretionary reasons. I would think you would be grateful," Tobias says.

"Of course they won't, because if anyone actually found out what has happened here they would have to look into it!"

Tobias sighs and gives me the same face I've been giving Griffin all night.

"Just listen to me for a minute, and then if you don't believe me I'll go and get in my car and you will never hear from me again," I plead.

"What? June—" Griffin starts to argue but I put my hand on his arm to quiet him.

"You are part of the Alliance that protects the Shield, right?" I ask. "Then you owe it to them— to the protection of that priceless artefact— to hear what I have to say."

Tobias looks at me, my hands on my hips, my eyes pleading with him.

He curses under his breath before sighing.

"I'm listening," he says.

"You know my Grandfather was accused of stealing the Shield twenty years ago, and he has always adamantly denied that it was there. But that wasn't true. The Shield was there; only it was taken right before his team opened the tomb. Someone who was involved with the dig stole it during the night and I don't know how, but they sold it to Charles for two hundred thousand pounds. Charles then sold it to someone else with the stipulation that they would have to donate it to the museum when the time was right, thus giving Charles the promotion of a lifetime," I pause, wondering if this little rant sounds as crazy as I think it does and look at Griffin, who nods at me encouragingly. "I think once Charles was able to reacquire the piece the thought of money outweighed his promotion, and so he stole it back again."

"That's a pretty wild theory," Ciara says, obviously amused.

"And this theory conveniently gets both you and your grandfather off the hook," Tobias says, nodding his head.

"There's just one problem: why would Charles steal it and then return it?"

"He was obviously under a lot of pressure from the Ashmolean. I think he thought he could blame it on me, but then when I started getting closer and closer to the truth he returned it before anything could be traced back to him."

Tobias looks at me before letting out a low whistle. "That's quite the story. And you have the proof to back all of this up?" he asks, though from his tone he clearly already knows the answer.

"I don't have any proof," I admit. "That's why I need to find out who Charles bought the piece from. If I can figure out who originally stole the shield, I'll have the proof I need."

"Just another wild goose chase," Tobias shakes his head. "I think I've followed you on enough of those these last few days."

He stands up straighter and gestures to the exit door at the end of the corridor. "We'll take you to your car now."

Looking from the Professor to Griffin I let out a frustrated breath. "Where's Max, he knows what has been going on, he can tell you that we're not crazy."

Ciara lets out a snort. "Good luck tracking that one down," she says. "He's been disappearing all over the place these last few days."

I decide to say nothing, as I don't want to get Max into any more trouble than I already have.

We open the back exit door at the end of the hallway and the alarm rings out.

"I told him to shut this off!" Tobias angrily spits out as he fishes his phone from his pocket.

"Much help he is," Ciara rolls her eyes. "You would think as a technology expert he would know how to reset the alarm. I think I should be havin' his job and he could chase you instead."

"What do you mean?" I ask her.

"When your grandpappy set off the alarm the other night, knockin' over that display case, I went to go and find Max and sure enough he was missin'. Charles came in screamin' that the alarm needed to be turned off, even tried to have a go on the computer himself but all he did was turn it up louder. All you had to do was press the alarm reset button in the security office. I managed in a few minutes once he got out of me way."

"You were the one that turned off the alarm?" I ask, turning the thought over in my head.

"That's what I just said," she frowns.

"Where was he— Max, I mean?" I ask.

"He said he was in this wings' security room. He thought the remote alarms were set up here for some reason, but he said all that was set up here were the surveillance cameras," Ciara rolls her eyes. "Not the brightest computer genius around."

"Oh my God," I say, looking to the Professor. "I know

what happened."

"Oh no, not another theory," Tobias rolls his eyes.

"Where is Charles?" I ask Ciara, ignoring Tobias.

"He's about to be sworn in as the new Curator," she answers, pointing to the main doorway to the Ashmolean.

"Of course he is."

Tobias reaches for my arm and starts to lead me. I look at Griffin, who nods before diving into Tobias's middle, tackling him to the ground.

"Get off!" Tobias yells, struggling to kick Griffin. I see Griffin's fake gun fall out of Tobias's pocket and onto the grass.

"I loved you in the Fanta commercials," the Professor winks at Ciara. "Had June go out and fetch me a whole case when I first watched it."

Griffin lets out a cry when Tobias's fist connects with his gut. Griffin tries to grab Tobias's face and push it down to the floor.

"That's it, I quit!" Ciara says, her head bent down to her chest as she shakes her head. "No one said I'd have to do combat."

Frowning at her odd behaviour, I hear Griffin yell out again and suddenly I remember what I am supposed to do.

"Hey, where are ya goin'?" Ciara yells as I bolt across the courtyard in front of the Ashmolean.

Chapter Twenty-Three

"Er– can I help you Ms Jenson?" the security guard that let me in that first day asks, peering over his desk as I frantically search the front atrium. He's got his bag and jacket in hand, so he must be about to leave.

"I need to speak to Charles– Mr Bringlett," I correct myself and try to appear a little less flustered. "Do you know where he is?"

"He's due in the press room in five minutes," he says, looking down at his watch. "I think he is in that room there getting ready."

He points to the administrative office on the far right.

"Thanks," I say, nodding and making my way over there.

"He actually didn't want to be disturbed," the security guard says, but my lack of response doesn't seem to bother him all that much.

Without knocking, I walk into the room and see Charles sitting at the desk, looking at the cue cards in his hand.

"Oh, for fuck's sake, June," he says, putting his cards down. "It's over. Let it go."

"No," I say, shaking my head. "It's not nearly over."

I look to my right as I close the door and notice a stone

statue sitting on a pedestal.

"Is that a bust of you?" I ask, looking a little closer. I notice the artist chiselled the nose a little crooked, which must be driving Charles crazy.

"All the curators have one, it's tradition. Actually, I'm about to be named head curator, so you'll excuse me if I don't have the time to hear your latest ramblings right now," Charles stands up and buttons his suit jacket

"Charles, just *listen* to me," I say, putting my hands on the edge of his desk. "Max stole the Shield."

He rolls his eyes before looking to the ceiling. "Who's next, June? First there was *no* Shield, then *I* stole the Shield, and now *Max*? You know what I think? I think the Professor actually found the Shield twenty years ago and when you saw it the other night you started on a full blown elaborate plot to confuse everyone."

"The Professor didn't take the Shield," I argue. "I think Max did."

"Max?" Charles snorts in disbelief. "That's ridiculous."

"He was in charge of the case, of the alarm for the Shield. Ciara herself told me that he was missing the whole time that it took for someone to steal the Shield. The camera footage is missing– I know he knows how to block out the cameras because he did it to get us in the building last night. He even took us up the same staircase he went down when he stole the Shield that night!"

Charles shakes his head in disbelief. "Why would Max

steal the Shield?"

"Because he was the one who sold it to you," I say. "He sold it to you and created the Alliance."

Charles laughs. "He didn't create the Alliance, June. It's *centuries* old."

"He told me that the night the Shield went missing, he went down to speak to the guard about the security systems, said the guard had no clue what to do when the alarms went off. Charles, when I left with the Professor I saw that guard and he was calling to see why the alarm had gone off. Max was nowhere near him!"

"That doesn't prove anything," Charles says.

"How do you know him?" I ask. "Why was he asked to be a part of the Alliance?"

"I met him a few years ago, at one of your Grandfather's lectures, actually," Charles says. "It was when I had lost that money, and I was asking for your help. The Professor was ill or something and you couldn't, so he helped me get it back from the bank. But I didn't ask him to be a part of the Alliance; the Alliance gave me his file and told me he was one of the recruits."

"I think Max created the Alliance, and used you as the recruitment officer because he saw first-hand when you lost that money that you don't tend to ask questions when things don't seem to make sense. How did you acquire the Shield?" I fire off the next question to him.

"Exactly like I told you," Charles shrugs. "I was

contacted by email about a piece they thought I would be interested in. The benefactor had already been in contact with the Alliance and they were the ones that suggested the Ashmolean would be the right place for the piece because I was already there to oversee it."

"Charles, the Alliance and the benefactor are the same person. There is no Alliance."

Charles shakes his head, but I can see the doubt starting to ebb its way in. Though I'm not entirely sure if it is because he believes me, or because he is beyond confused.

"Tobias isn't ex-military. And Ciara is an actress from the Fanta commercials," I say.

He opens his mouth to argue, but then frowns. "But why would he steal the Shield *after* he donated it?"

"I think that's why he had me join the Alliance. He wanted to see how I would react to seeing the Shield and if I would accept the discovery of it."

"I don't follow," Charles says.

"If I reacted as though it meant nothing to me, then he was fine. The Shield could be donated and no one would be the wiser of his involvement, he could carry on as planned," I say. "But when he saw that I wasn't taking it well, he needed to steal it, he needed to cast doubt on me so that if I ever kicked up a fuss about the Shield or started to ask questions, no would believe me."

"Believe you about what?" Charles asks.

"When I started asking about where the Shield has been

for twenty years and who originally stole it."

"You think Max stole it from Sutton-Hoo?" Charles says, laughing. "He would have been a boy."

"No, he didn't steal it," I shake my head.

"He did steal it, he didn't steal it, this is all just speculation that makes no sense," Charles shakes his head before picking up his cue cards. "June, you have to stop this. The Shield is in the museum, where it belongs. No one knows you had anything to do with this; I've kept your name out of everything. It doesn't matter who did what or when. It's *over*, let it go."

"I can't let it go," I say, throwing my hands in the air. "I'm not going to stop until I have the answers I'm looking for."

"So you are going to accuse Max of stealing the Shield when he was what... ten years old? Then try to convince everyone he came up with an elaborate scheme to donate and then steal the Shield back?"

"No. Because Max didn't steal the Shield twenty years ago," I say.

"June's right," I turn as I hear his voice behind me. Max is standing in the doorway pointing a gun at me. I'd like to say the sight is shocking, but to be honest, I've seen so many guns in the past few days they've lost a little of the shock for me.

"Max, what's going on?" Charles yells in outrage

Max puts his finger to his lips before closing the door

behind him. "Please, Charles, June was about to reveal my secret."

"You didn't steal the Shield," I say, studying his face. "Your grandfather did."

Max smiles. "You figured it out. I knew you would."

"So you framed me," I guess.

"I didn't want to. I think it's important that you know that," Max says, looking slightly regretful before he shrugs. "Unfortunately, your persistence for answers left me very little choice in the matter. Every time I spoke to you, you unravelled more and more of a plan that took me *years* to come up with. In days!"

"Why you little snake–" Charles starts but Max raises the gun in his direction.

"I think it might be better if you let the grownups chat here," Max says, returning his attention to me, and I feel Charles bristle at the comment.

"It does help that everyone already thinks your grandfather is off his rocker. But you– people respect you, June. They respect your intelligence. If you went off on a rambling about the Shield I'm sure a lot of the sheep would have just thrown you in with your grandfather, but I think you would cause a few to stop and think for a minute as well."

"Your grandfather was a volunteer on the Professor's excavation team," I say. "My grandfather wrote about him in his journal, how excited he was at the prospect of discovering treasure."

"My grandfather loved archaeology, dug all over our property, always hoping he would find something," Max remembers fondly. "When he came home from that excavation, he showed me the Shield. He had opened the tomb by himself– there wasn't a lot of security back then. Can you believe he just took it home in his suitcase? I knew where it had come from of course. I knew he had stolen it. Even at such a young age, I thought it was unlikely the university let their volunteers take souvenirs home. The man was impossible when he was drinking, though. At first I tried to tell him he had to hand it in to the museum, that it belonged somewhere that people could preserve it, study it, and appreciate it."

"But he wouldn't," I state the obvious.

"He was a stubborn man, I certainly don't have to tell you what that's like. He hid it somewhere. I searched all over for years, but could never find it. There were holes all over the property from where he had dug for his own treasure hunting– he owned nearly a hundred acres and it really could have been in any of them. There was a moment at the end, when he wasn't well, that I convinced him to turn it over and he told me where it was. But then the newspapers reported that your grandfather might have stolen the Shield from the tomb. I saw them drag his name through the mud, and I just couldn't let them do that to my grandfather, to our family."

"But it was more than fine that they did it to mine!" I say, the anger coursing through me with his every word.

"I was just going to donate it anonymously, but it was all over the news at that time; I knew people would start asking questions. I sat in on one of your grandfather's lectures when he spoke about how museums preserve artefacts, and it was actually very helpful. I went up to you after class to ask you a question, but you ran after the Professor in such a hurry. That's when I met Charles," he nods in Charles's direction. "I knew he was your friend, I'd seen you two together, so I made a feeble joke about women running away at the sight of me and we started chatting."

"And he told you that he was missing some money," I say, shaking my head because that is exactly the topic Charles would choose to discuss with a total stranger.

"Actually I overheard him tell you, so I told him I could help recover it for him, look into who stole it. I managed to get it back for him– it was a simple fraud case– and was shocked he didn't seem to even care who had taken it. I remember thinking he would be a lovely scape goat."

"You little–" Charles mutters.

Max points the gun at Charles again and raises his eyebrows. Charles seems to back down and Max returns his attention to me.

"So when the time came for me to donate the piece to the museum, I needed to know what was going to be done with it. To keep my ear close to the grindstone, as they say,

244

in case people started to question the benefactor. Of course, there are anonymous donations to the museum all the time, but this one I was sure might raise a few eyebrows, given its history."

"So you recruited Charles to lead the Alliance, and then got yourself recruited as well," I nod. "And Ciara and Tobias?"

"Ciara I met in one of my acting classes at Cambridge— never known someone who could stay in character better. She thinks this is a reality series, I've given her a pin that she thinks is a microphone," Max laughs. "Tobias is a security guard from Asda. He thinks there really is an Alliance, poor fool, just tired of chasing down people who've nicked pork pies I suppose."

"But you didn't recruit me," I point out. "I asked Charles to join."

"Yes, that was a little trickier, but I did plan it that way. I knew you would never take it at face value like the others. I would leave books on the table before you were about to sit down in the library that eluded to a secret Alliance— all conspiracy theorists mind you. When I met with Charles to discuss joining the Alliance he mentioned that you were visiting later so I left a folder on the desk all about the secret society. I knew you would be intrigued."

It's annoying how spot on he really is.

"But I knew you were the final piece. You were the only one who would have looked into the Shield— others of course would try but I was very careful covering my tracks– but I knew the lack of proof wouldn't stop you," Max says. "Forging the letters of authenticity wasn't hard. I mean, I knew the Shield was real so it would hold up if it was ever questioned or studied. I watched your reaction very carefully when you first saw the Shield, you were clearly shaken, but almost detached. I actually thought for a minute you might accept it for what it was. But then I heard you speaking to Charles in the hallway. I listened to you over the security system and I knew then that you wouldn't stop. You'd raised all the questions I had feared you would."

"So you stole the Shield?" Charles asks, obviously confused. "What was the point of that?"

"Because my grandfather would always be under suspicion where the Shield is concerned, and no one would ever listen to him. Max needed to make sure no one would ever believe me either," I explain.

"You are smart," he smiles. "It actually worked out better than I could have hoped. With you running away everyone's focus was on you. No one even questioned where I was or what I was doing when it was stolen. I thought you would run and hide, but yet again you wouldn't give up. You started digging, asking more and more questions about the Shield and where it had come from."

"There's one thing I don't understand," I say. "Why did you put the Shield back?"

"I always wanted the Shield in the museum. I may not

have a doctorate in it, but I can understand the importance of artefacts to our history. My grandfather did too, if it wasn't for the drinking he never would have done what he did," Max explains. "I'm not a terrible person, June, I am trying to do the right thing here. But you've left me no choice, I'm afraid."

"No choice for what?"

"If I thought– even for a *moment*– that you would let this go, I could let you live," Max genuinely looks troubled by the whole thing.

"I can let it go," Charles offers. I shoot him a nasty look.

"I promise you, June, I will make sure your grandfather gets the proper care he needs," Max says.

"Max you're not thinking this through clearly," I try and explain. "There are other people that know what has happened. There are other people that will be asking questions."

"They'll let it go," he says, almost reassuring himself. "They don't know what you know. You didn't know everything until I told you."

I study his face and see that he is starting to get agitated. I think the thought of killing me– of putting an end to this– was a lot easier in theory for him. Now that he actually has to carry out the plan, I can see the hesitation in his movements.

"What about our bodies?" I question him. "Surely someone will question our deaths. They'll hear the gun shots!"

"It's a simple matter of self-preservation," Max says, as though this is the least of his worries. "You accused Charles and he shot you. I came into the room after I saw you come in here and fought the gun out of Charles's hand before killing him in self-defence. And the gun has a silencer."

His hand is shaking heavily on the gun pointed at me and I start to get worried that any movement from me and he might pull the trigger on instinct.

"Max, I can help you," I say, trying to calm him down. "You haven't really done anything wrong. You've stolen something that technically already belonged to you, anyways."

I see his eyes start to shift side to side as he looks down for a moment, thinking things through.

"You don't want to hurt anybody," I say, taking a step towards him. "You were just trying to protect your grandfather. Your family."

"Don't come any closer," he says, raising the gun higher again.

"Max, please, I only want to help you. I will talk to the authorities, and Charles will speak to the museum," I look at Charles, who nods eagerly, never taking his eyes off the gun.

"It's too late," Max says, looking at me with tears in his eyes. "I didn't want to hurt you, June. I know what you've been through. I've been through it too. I loved my grandfather."

My eyes widen as I see the door open behind him, and the Professor enters the room. He's moved so quietly, and with Max lost in his own thoughts, no one else seems to have heard him come in.

"I'm sorry, June," Max says, as though he's finally made his decision. "I wish there was another way."

He points the gun directly at my chest, but at the same time the Professor whacks him on the top of his head with the butt of the gun in his hand. Max's body crumples to the floor.

"This is a bloody good prop, I'd say," the Professor says, looking down at the gun in his hand. "Very substantial."

I quickly run over to Max and pick up the gun that has fallen out of his hand.

"Professor, what are you doing here? Where are Griffin and the others?"

"Our young driver is still wrestling out front with the big brute. The rest of us got a bit tired of watching, to be honest, so we thought we'd come and find you."

"How did you know we were in here?" I ask.

"Didn't. Looking for the gift shop, actually," he says, shaking his head. "You know I'm starting to think there isn't any whiskey left in all of bloody England."

He waves his arm to the side for emphasis, and knocks Charles's bust off the pedestal.

"Oh for fuck's sake," Charles makes his way over to the bust, the head now separated from the neck. "That took weeks to make."

"The nose is crooked," the Professor points out. "Might want to get them to fix that on the next one."

Chapter Twenty-Four

Standing in the kitchen I arrange the little sandwiches and tarts onto the tray, trying to balance the plate with the weight of the teapot.

Behind me I hear the rattle of the glass panes as the door leading to the cobblestone patio in the garden opens. Looking over my shoulder I see the Professor amble through, closing the door with a thud and I wince for the poor glass.

"Your young chap is bloody impatient out there for his tea," the Professor says, walking over to the tray and removing a sandwich. "Never heard someone go on so much in my whole bloody life."

I fight the urge to roll my eyes.

"Be a dear and put a shot of whiskey in there for an old man," he pleads, nodding to his teacup.

"It's not even one o'clock!" I say, looking at my watch.

"June, when you get to be my age you must learn to live every minute as though it could be your last," he proclaims. "Now wouldn't you feel just terrible if you knew this could be my last chance for a spot?"

"Fine," I agree. "But if Ruth invites us round for tea

tonight you're coming, and you'll be on your best behaviour."

The Professor frowns before shrugging his shoulder. "Fine, but I'm going to be a right pain in the ass for the rest of the day to make up for it, then."

I smile and then kiss him on the cheek. "I'd be disappointed if you weren't."

"You know, he is a decent fellow," the Professor says, indicating the patio door. "You could have done worse. It will be nice to have you fussing over someone else for a change."

"Well, thank you for that encouragement," I reply.

"I think I'll take my tea in the study, after all," he says, taking a few more sandwiches and a tart off of the tray.

"You need a plate!" I argue, taking one off the counter and handing it to him to pile his food on. "You don't want to eat with us?"

"Can't June Bug, have to prepare for next week. Daniel and I are doing a week long seminar on the dig," he says this like he hasn't told me every moment, of every day, for the last three weeks. "Bloody came crawling back, didn't they?"

The completely satisfied look on his face brings a smile to mine, no matter how many times I hear it.

"Sure we can't tempt you to join us?" he says, raising his eyebrows. "They'll naturally have questions about the acquisition of the Shield."

"No, thank you. I think I've talked about it far more than I'd like already," I say. "Besides, I've got my own classes next week and I'll already have to fend off questions from them."

"Everyone loves the hero of the hour," he says to me, biting into one of the sandwiches.

"They should be talking to you then," I say, shaking my head. "You're the one who saved the day."

"Nonsense, the only thing I did was knock the poor bugger out," the Professor argues.

"And saved mine and Charles's lives," I point out. "I wouldn't be alive today if it weren't for you."

The Professor smiles at me.

"The great ones, June Bug, don't live for today, they live for eternity," The Professor picks up his teacup with his other hand. "Something to think about."

He walks out of the kitchen with his plate of sandwiches and tea and leaves me in the kitchen.

Carrying the tray, I open the back door and make my way over to the small table set up in the garden.

"Oh, thank God," Griffin says, picking up a sandwich the minute the tray is on the table. "I'm absolutely starving."

"I'd heard," I muse, watching him devour the tiny sandwich in two bites.

"Did he tell you the alumni called him about his teaching series next week? Basically made them beg to have him back again, even though he's been working on his lectures all week." Griffin has a grin of appreciation on his face. "Maybe that's the approach I should take."

"Still haven't decided who to go with, then?" I ask. "I thought you decided on that lady from London who was going to give you the money for the play and free reign?"

"I was," he hedges. "You know final decisions aren't my strong point."

Nodding, I pick up my teacup and take a sip as Griffin's phone rings in his pocket, causing him to groan.

"I bet it's the bloody alumni calling again," he says, shaking his head. "You know he's given them *my* mobile number."

"We had to turn the ringer off in the house, the Professor says it gives him a headache," I say. I've actually been enjoying the peace and quiet in the house considering the phone has been ringing off the hook the past few weeks.

Griffin takes out the phone from his pocket, looking at the screen.

"Oh, no, it's only Mum," he says and presses the TALK button.

I try to keep my expression as pleasant as possible as I pick up a sandwich from the tray and take a bite while Griffin talks to his Mum.

Honestly, there might be a few separation issues there. Ruth calls him– a lot. Which is fine, I know what caring for a loved one entails, so I fully appreciate his relationship with his mother. It's the relationship that she seems to want with me I find just a little unnerving.

I mean, I know I sound unreasonable. I've never really

had a mother-type figure so I should be really grateful for all the love and attention.

But it's really hard to remember that when she keeps showing up at my lectures in her curlers telling me she's packed a lunch in case I forget to eat.

Which sounds really sweet, but she brought it in front of all two hundred of my students in the lecture hall, and proceeded to let me how she's managed to work out the spaghetti stain on my trousers from the night before. She basically ripped them off my legs at the dinner table. I had to go home in one of her nightgowns.

Also, I think the students have started calling me Professor Boyardee behind my back.

Griffin hangs up the phone and smiles.

"Mum invited us around for tea. She made the Professor his lemon cookies," he says, smiling at me before turning to collect some more sandwiches off of the tray.

"Lovely," I nod.

"Have you seen this," he says, pointing at the paper that is sitting at the far edge of the table.

I shake my head, picking the paper up to see Max's face on the front page. It looks like they've used his class photo from Oxford. The headline reads: *Things Nearly Turn Deadly at The Ashmolean*. I've been following the case for the last few weeks in the paper, and although Griffin reminds me it is terribly irrational considering he tried to frame me for a crime before he attempted to kill me, a part of me can't help but feel sorry for Max.

"He pled guilty to attempted murder," Griffin says, looking at me. "You won't have to testify now."

"I know," I say, nodding my head. "How long do you think he'll get?"

"With this system? He'll probably be out in the morning," Griffin shakes his head. "Surely at least ten to fifteen years."

I nod my head, looking down into my cup of tea.

"Let's not dwell on it," he says, covering my hand with his and offering me a smile. "Daniel called earlier when you were inside and said the Professor did marvellous last week at the press conferences. Only tried to take his trousers off once."

I laugh at the image of Dr Cooke trying to convince the Professor to keep his trousers on in the middle of the Ashmolean.

"They used to call it the erratic behaviour of a mad man," I say, shaking my head. "Now they all find it endearing."

"Enjoy it, June," he says, putting his arm around me. "You deserve this. You both do."

"I spoke to Charles," I say, and immediately see Griffin's back stiffen. "He says hello."

Griffin offers me a smile before biting into another sandwich. I can't be sure but I think I hear the word 'git' before he takes a bite. Griffin and Charles haven't quite become friends yet. It's probably because of the whole

Charles sending-people-to-get-me-to-try-and-confess-to-a-crime-I-didn't-commit thing.

I've let it go though, so I don't see why he can't. Well, I've almost let it go. I have to let Charles sweat for a bit, or it just wouldn't be right. The Professor taught me that.

"So is this the one you've decided on then?" I ask Griffin, pointing to the bound playbook beside him.

"I think so," he sighs, but doesn't look entirely convinced.

"Have you written the ending?" I ask.

He nods.

"Well, go on. How does it end?" I lean forward to grab it.

He quickly picks it up and puts it high in the air, away from my grasp. He looks at my eager face and smiles, obviously loving the fact I want to know so badly.

"Just as it should," he says and brings his lips to mine.

ABOUT THE AUTHOR

Emily Harper is the bestselling women's fiction author of White Lies, Checking Inn, My Sort-of, Kind-of Hero and the June Jenson series. Her debut novel, White Lies, was a finalist in the National Excellence in Romantic Fiction award. My Sort-of, Kind-of Hero won the RWA Book Buyer's Best award as well as the Reader's Choice award.

Originally from England, she currently lives in Canada with her family and is working on June's next adventure.

June Jenson's adventure continues in

June Jenson
and the Coins of Cassidy

Available Now

Chapter One

"Where does this one go?" Griffin peers over the side of the box at me.

"Er—" I look down at the piece of paper in my hand and squint. "I think storage."

"Storage?" Griffin frowns and peers inside the box, causing his floppy brown hair to fall across his forehead. "It has all my toiletries!"

"Right, that must be a six, not an eight," I say, looking down at the list again through dark rimmed glasses. "Box twenty-six is the bathroom."

"Can I not just look in the boxes and figure it out? This is taking forever!" he complains. His eyes look helpless and between that and his dishevelled hair, it's difficult for me to stay irritated with him.

Difficult, but not impossible.

"No, or the whole number system will be for nothing!"

Honestly, he's been a pain in my side all day.

Griffin mumbles under his breath as he walks past me to the staircase. I manage to catch: "Already bloody waste of time", and I actively choose to ignore it.

Compromise. That's what all great relationships thrive

on—or so I'm told. The truth is, being in a loving relationship isn't as easy as I thought it was going to be, especially when your significant other drives you up the wall most of the time. I mean he tries—bless him, he *really* tries—and I should appreciate the effort and not focus on the fact he makes a right mess of things. It's something I'm working on. To be honest, the main problem might be that neither of us have a clue what we're doing. We are the wrong side of thirty and this is the first real relationship either of us has ever been in.

"June, look what I've just found!" The Professor comes out of his study with his woolly vest neatly buttoned for a change and holds up a long pair of needle nose pliers.

"Er—wonderful," I volunteer, and return to study my list. I don't know why I keep looking at it; it's a complete mess. I can't make out anything that is written for a combination of reasons: one being the Professor spilled his tea all over it, and the other being Griffin has the worst handwriting I've ever seen. My eidetic memory would have been able to memorize it if he hadn't insisted on writing it all out himself. Another "helpful" effort.

"I think I'll label them," the Professor says, his light blue eyes magnified by his rimless spectacles. He glances at the scattered boxes in the front entry. "Where's my bloody label maker?"

"Professor, I thought we agreed you were going to cut back on the labelling?"

"I have cut back! I'm only labelling the important things," the Professor argues.

"They're pliers," I say. "We have another three pairs in the shed!"

"But these are the ones that I used to get the Monopoly boot out of your nose," he says. "Don't want to forget that."

I look at the dirty pliers in his hand, covered in rust.

He's been doing well lately, much better days than I could have hoped for, especially in this later stage of Alzheimer's. The medication is working just as it should, but he's still slipping away from me. It's gradual, which is both a blessing and a curse. Before, we would have good days and bad days. It was very black and white. Now, everything seems to be grey. The days go by smoothly, he forgets things here and there, and the episodes where he can't remember who he is are not quite as dramatic as they once were. But he does forget things. Little things that seem of no significance: where his coat is, or if he turned a light off. They all seem insignificant, but everyday some new little thing is added to the list and the tally is getting long.

"Right, what about number thirty-three?" Griffin says, picking up a box from beside my foot.

"Umm…" I squint at the paper but I can't see any thirty-three anywhere. "That's for the… er… bedroom."

Griffin narrows his eyes at me but doesn't say anything as he goes back up the stairs.

"The label maker?" the Professor asks me.

"Oh, right, well… it's umm…" I push my unruly chin length brown hair away from my face and tuck the curling strands behind my ear while I look around at the foyer for the tiny blue machine. Amidst all the boxes it's hard to make out where anything is. "It should be around here somewhere."

"Absolute mess," the Professor says, shaking his head. "I've only seen that lad wear two shirts. Where did all his bloody stuff come from?"

I look around and wonder myself. There is no way all of this stuff used to fit into Griffin's bedroom. I roll up the sleeves of my oversized jumper and open the lid of the box closest to me.

"Ha! I caught you!" Griffin yells from the top of the staircase. The heel of his boot slips on the edge of the step, and he slips down a few steps before he grabs the railing to right himself. "Finally admitting defeat on your chart, I see."

"What is *this* doing here?" I say, reaching into the box and pulling out a purple floral lampshade. "This is from your Mum's sitting room!"

"Is it?" Griffin says, but I see the guilty look on his face before he's able to hide it.

I pull back the lid more and my eyes widen. "This is her soup ladle!"

"What? How did that get in there?" he asks, grabbing it from my hand and placing it back in the box. "Must have just got mixed up with all the commotion of packing."

Ignoring him, I walk over to another box and lift the lid. "She's packed you her microwave!"

I push that box aside and lift the lid of the next one.

"Why did your mother pack up her Barbara Streisand CDs?" I narrow my eyes at Griffin.

"It's probably just a misunderstanding. You know Mum, she's a bit flighty," Griffin says, picking up the box. "I'll get them out of the way until we can sort it all out."

"Just put it back in the car," I put my hands on my hips. "We can just drive it back over to her house."

"Right, of course," Griffin says, but doesn't make a move for the doorway. "You know, maybe I will just put them in storage for now and once we get more settled I'll take them back to her."

"It's okay, I have to nip out in a minute," I argue. "I'll drop them off for her."

I try and take the box out of Griffin's hands, but he holds on tight.

"You don't have to do that," he says.

"Yes, I think I do," I say.

"Honestly, it's only a couple of CDs," he argues.

"Is it though?" I ask, stepping away from the box to open another by his feet. "Oh look! Her dressing gown and slippers!"

I pick them up out of the box and hold them up for Griffin to see.

"Right, you know, there might have been something I've

been meaning to tell you..." he starts.

"Which is?"

"Well, you know how Mum took it when I finally told her I was moving out," Griffin says. "She was a bit upset."

"She cried for three weeks and is now on Xanax," I correct him.

"Exactly, the poor thing," Griffin drops the box and sidles up a bit closer to me.

I look to the Professor, who stands with his lips pursed. He's not Ruth's biggest fan. At first he was able to tolerate her, but then two weeks ago she took his label maker without asking and all hell broke loose.

Of course the Professor says he remembers none of it: the shouting, the ridiculing of the curlers. He even had a go at her scones.

I'd swear on my last dying breath he remembers every word.

"I told her I would visit her, that she wouldn't even notice I was gone." Griffin puts his hands on my arms as though trying to calm me down. "And, of course, she's over the moon she has you to fuss over now as well."

I will my face to remain neutral.

"She was a right mess last week when she was packing all of my stuff up—you should have seen her—absolutely inconsolable."

"Get to the point about the CDs," I say through gritted teeth.

"Well she was packing up my stuff when she—er—*we* remembered she hadn't been on holiday for a while."

I raise one eyebrow.

"So I thought it would be nice for her to take a bit of time for herself and get away from it all," he smiles.

"So why is her stuff here?" I ask. "It's not like she's moving."

"Right, she's not moving. I want you to keep that thought foremost in your mind," he says.

"Griffin," I say slowly, trying to keep my pulse steady. "Where is your mother going on holiday?"

"Well, she can't fly because of her knees," he says. "And the buses are out because of that, too. She can't go on the train because she says there's too many knife crimes on them."

"No, absolutely not," I shake my head.

"Where is she going?" the Professor interjects, still holding his pliers.

"Your mother is not staying here!" I practically yell, and watch Griffin's face fall.

"Why not? It will only be for a few weeks. A month, tops," he argues.

"No! Absolutely not," I'm still shaking my head. "What's the point of you moving out if your mother is just going to move in here with you?"

"First of all, she's not *moving* in here with me. She's coming to stay as my *guest*. I am allowed to have guests, am

I not?"

"Not ones that are still trying to nurse you," I say, picking the box back up off of the floor.

"It's not as if it's forever," Griffin says, following me as I walk to the doorway. "It's only until her nerves calm down."

"Her nerves are never going to calm down!" I say, shaking my head at him. "She just uses them to keep her hold on you."

"That is completely unfair!" Griffin says, putting his arm across the doorway to stop me from leaving.

"Really?" I raise my eyebrows. "So if your Mum is just coming for a visit, why does she need the entire contents of her house?"

He looks at the boxes and frowns slightly. "This stuff reminds her of my dad. She likes to have them around her so she doesn't forget him."

"We got her that microwave for Christmas. How does that remind her of your dad?" I ask.

"What if I tell her she can only stay for a week?" he suggests. "She just wants to help out while I get really stuck in with the screenplay."

I briefly close my eyes.

Griffin's play, which he'd been working on for the good part of a decade, was a huge success. I think the person most surprised with this result was Griffin considering he'd called off the production about ten times before opening night, thinking it was all rubbish. The reviews came in and they were glowing. Critics asked when they could see more of his work. After a year with sold out shows, a producer approached him and offered him a deal to turn it into a screenplay. It should have been fantastic news, but Griffin came home from the meeting in a cold sweat. And so began the anxiety: how was he ever going to repeat the play's success in film format. It's been nearly six months since they signed the deal and he's written nothing. Did I mention the first draft was due two weeks ago?

Honestly, I want to be supportive about this. I am *desperately* trying to be supportive. But it's all too much right now. Between moving in together, his mother's constant hovering, and the Professor labelling the entire contents of our house, I am not sure how much more of this I can take.

I may not be an expert on men—Griffin being my first real boyfriend and my best friend Charles accusing me of stealing the Shield of Quell to save his own skin—but I do not think this is normal male behaviour.

"Griffin, if your mother steps across that threshold she will never leave!"

"You are being unreasonable," he says and looks to the Professor for help. The Professor offers up nothing, and still looks shocked at the idea of Ruth staying here.

"How am I being unreasonable? For not wanting my boyfriend's mother to come and live with me?" I ask, pushing my glasses further up the bridge of my nose while balancing the box with my hip.

"She's not living with us, it's a *holiday*," Griffin argues. "And plus, I don't really see what the big deal is."

I look at the Professor, who stares back at me with wide eyes. It's very subtle, but I see him frantically shaking his head at me.

"How could this not be a big deal?" I say to Griffin.

I will myself to stay calm and try and see this from his point of view, but the more I look at Ruth's dressing gown poking out of the box, the more I want to throw all of her stuff onto the front lawn.

"We're moving in here with the Professor," Griffin says. "So what's the difference if we also live with my Mum for a bit?"

"Oh good God, it is *so* not the same thing!"

"How is it not?"

"Because, the Professor isn't well. I can't just *not* take care of him," I say this slowly to try and make him understand.

"Mum's not well either," Griffin says, trying a new tactic.

I open my mouth to argue, but then close it. I just don't know what to say anymore. Sometimes it feels so hopeless, and I have no idea how we got here. How *I* got here.

I have spent my entire adult life trying to get out of the shadow of my grandfather and the accusations of him stealing a relic from his dig site at Sutton Hoo. I thought once he was proven innocent, I would be free. Free from the whispers, free from the limitations in my work, free to live my life the way I want to live it. And really none of those things have happened.

Of course there were apologies all around, but the truth is you can never erase what has been done. We are no longer cast as the family who stole a priceless relic; now we are the family that was accused and exonerated of the crime. The page in history isn't wiped clean, and it never will be. The whispering has somewhat died away, but it was replaced with reporters hounding us for interviews, begging us for our side of the story. Our faces were plastered over the tabloids for months, and reporters still show up unannounced for a comment. What they don't seem to understand is: we don't want to talk about the scandal; we only want to talk about the history. How can I move forward when all anyone wants to do is look back?

I continue to teach Introductory to Ancient Artefacts at Oxford, but I want to discover new history– I want to have an adventure that is my own. I've applied to multiple excavation sites– not even for the lead archaeologist position. I am willing to work any position. And every time I have been denied. I know Oxford isn't happy with the articles in the tabloids. They've made me do numerous interviews and press tours on behalf of the university in an attempt to repair their image, but never seem to be happy with the outcome. Somewhere it's always written that they didn't believe us, or they might have been involved with the cover up. And somehow I get blamed for it—very discreetly of course. *It's not the right kind of publicity*, or so I've overheard. A month ago I asked the university to submit my name to a site, as they've done for countless Professors and Assistants, and they came back and offered me a guest lecture tour in some little town in Russia instead. They just want me out of their bloody hair, but can't fire me because of the negative publicity it would cause. Somehow they've managed to think of themselves as the victim in all of this when they were the ones who falsely accused my grandfather and exiled him to a life of early retirement.

And the bloody tabloids don't help. At first they were very supportive of our family and how we'd been wronged, and made Oxford out to be the pompous monsters. Then the story became old and they started hounding us for an exclusive interview. It's very difficult to repeatedly tell someone to sod off while hoping they don't turn on you for it. A reporter from the Daily Journal, Simon Locke, would wait for me to leave the house, to try and approach the Professor. He'd corner him in the shops when Griffin and I weren't looking. It started to get to the point we couldn't let the Professor out of our sights. Not that the Professor would purposefully say something wrong, it's just—well, last week he thought he was Sean Connery, so who knows what he's likely to say.

So, the tabloids turned on me, the bastards. I mean, I know I really shouldn't expect a lot from the people who try to get the latest shot of an actress without her top on, but for a moment it was nice to feel like someone was finally on my family's side. They started printing pictures of the Professor with his trousers down, speculating about how I was able to figure things out with the Shield of Quell unless I was involved in the coverup. They even tried to chalk up Griffin's involvement with the Shield as a publicity stunt to plug his play. Of course, the tabloids never come out and say anything for fear of a slander suit, but they sure are pros at insinuation.

And all it's served to do is bugger up my chances of ever having a dig site of my own. Even when I threatened to leave and take a position at another university, Oxford didn't budge. I might have been able to get away with it at first, but after the tabloids turned on me I didn't have much pull. Somehow I've gained a reputation in the archaeology community as a glory seeker, and now *no one* wants to work with me.

And then there's Griffin. I love him. I *really* do. And we aren't a normal couple—I know that. We both have responsibilities that we can't just toss aside, and for all of Ruth's faults I know that Griffin needs her just as much as she needs him. I just don't want this to be another thing in my life that has limitations.

Also, it would be nice if he didn't leave his bath towel on the floor every single morning.

"I thought you wanted to move in with me. I thought

we had decided that this was the next step in our relationship," I say.

"I do! Of course I do." He takes the box out of my hands and places it on the ground. "You know I want us to be together more than anything."

He wraps his arms around me and I settle against his chest.

"Please tell her she can't come," I say to him, trying not to let the desperation come through in my voice.

I need this to work out right now. I just need one thing in my life to move forward.

He kisses the top of my head and sighs.

"Okay, I'll tell her she can't stay here."

"Ruth. Not. Coming. To. Stay," the Professor says out loud as he writes in the brown leather journal he uses as a memory prompt. "The. Lad. Has. Whiskey. In. Box. Eighteen."

Griffin and I smile at each other. He brings his lips to mine, and I wrap my arms around his neck.

"Ugh hmm," a voice says from behind me.

I turn to see Dr Cooke standing on the front steps with amusement on his face.

"Nothing like young love is there, Albert?" Dr Cooke looks at the Professor, who is still holding the pliers tightly to his chest. "Perhaps that's why the great writers always try and capture it's glory."

"Hmm," the Professor idly nods in agreement.

"Though, I believe most writers find the tragedy of love to be the most compelling theme. Romeo and Juliet, Tristan and Isolde, Anthony and Cleopatra…"

I look at the Professor and frown.

"Paris and Helena, Cathy and Heathcliff–"

"Right, wonderful," I say, cutting off the Professor's list. "I think we get the idea."

"I think I read a paper on that a few weeks ago…" the Professor says, before turning and wandering back through the hallway and into his study.

"Cheery mood today, I see," Dr Cooke says and Griffin and I motion him to follow us into the Professor's study.

We find the Professor at his desk, shuffling through a stack of papers.

"I could have sworn I put it in this pile," he says looking at the stack of papers perched precariously on the edge of his desk. "Yes, I even labelled this pile as interesting material."

"Never mind about that paper, Albert," Dr Cooke says, waving the envelopes he has in his hand. "I've got much more exciting things for you to read."

The Professor's eyes light up at the sight of them, and I frown.

"What's all this about?" I ask, pointing at the envelopes.

I usually get the post myself, making sure to sift through the letters and remove the never ceasing requests from the press. I don't want him to see any of them during one his episodes and call the reporters. That bloody Simon Locke is starting to get creative, and makes the envelopes look like the Professor has won something. They *say* they want to know our side of the story, but I know better than to trust those trying to sell papers.

"These are the applications for the internship we are offering," Dr Cooke explains.

"Internship?" I ask. "What do you two need an intern for?"

They both look up at me and frown.

"My dear, we are *very* busy men. Think of all we could accomplish if we no longer have to do the mundane tasks of life," Dr Cooke reasons.

I can't help the snort that escapes. "You two spent all day yesterday labelling the jelly you made over the weekend."

"And we could have been making important discoveries if we didn't have to label those jars ourselves," the Professor argues.

"How did you even get approval for this?" I ask. "You're not even on staff at the University anymore!"

"This isn't through the University," Dr Cooke waves away my question. "Privately funded."

"Oh no," I say. "What have you two been up to?"

"Too soon to get into details, June Bug," the Professor taps the side of his nose. "Let's just say we have a lot to teach the youth of today, and the academic community is finally getting their heads out of their arses."

"Now I'm genuinely worried," I say, coming to stand

closer to the desk.

"I wouldn't mind an intern," Griffin says, sitting in the armchair. "Make my tea, do my laundry…"

"Then what would your mother do?" I snap at him before turning back to the Professor. "You realize that you would actually have to mentor this person—you can't just have your own personal slave, you know."

"June, I'm offended you think so little of us," Dr Cooke shakes his head. "We plan on teaching our new intern all we know about the world of Archaeology."

"God only knows how much time we have left," the Professor chimes in. "It would be a shame to waste the knowledge and experience that we have dedicated our lives to acquiring."

I stare at the two of them, not buying a single word of it.

"I was partial to that one," Dr Cooke holds up a peach coloured envelope. "He says he can walk a tightrope. That's bound to come in useful at some point."

"You two never leave this house!" I shake my head. "When would you need someone to tightrope walk for you?"

"Always be prepared, June Bug," the Professor mumbles as he reads the CV.

"Oh, June, this one's for you," Dr Cooke hands me a white envelope. "Found it on the floor by the post box."

I look down at the envelope and frown. It's from Oxford, and it's thick. That can't be good.

I turn the envelope over and slide my finger under the

top seal. I take the pages out, unfold them, and begin reading.

Dear Professor Jenson,

We hope that you are enjoying your summer holidays and trust that everyone is well. We are writing to inform you that this coming term we would like to offer you the position of Head of Archaeology at Oxford University. As you are aware, Dr Phillip Hurst is currently the department head, but we have had notice from the American Historical Society in the United States of America that his presence is required in Colorado at the beginning of the term on an exciting potential find involving none other than the notorious Butch Cassidy! As you may know, Dr Hurst is currently away and unreachable on a soul searching expedition in the Congo Jungle with the Nanuba tribe. We have not yet been able to reach him, but we are confident that we will be able to do so in time.

If, for some unknown reason, we are not able to contact Dr Hurst, he will continue to fulfil his position as Department Head, and in which case we would need to kindly rescind this offer. Naturally, when Dr Hurst returns from the United States you would return to your current position with Oxford University. We hope that this offer will meet with your approval and that you will find it both challenging and fulfilling to your professional development.

Regards,

William Dockery

Associate Dean

Oxford University

"The cheek!" I yell, looking up at the men in the room.

I look down at the letter again and commit it to memory, shaking my head in disgust. That's it. This is the last, final, bloody straw.

"What's wrong?" the Professor asks, frowning.

"Phillip Hurst, that's what's wrong!" I cry in outrage, crumpling the papers and flinging them into the waste basket.

"Phillip Hurst?" Griffin asks. "The bloke with the nice hair?"

I scowl in his direction.

Perfect hair. Perfect career. Perfect bloody life. He's been an archaeologist for all of five seconds. And in that five seconds (alright, eight years and two months, but who's *really* counting?) he's managed to be a part of all of these amazing excavations that have brought great press to Oxford. He's talented, wealthy (his great-great grandfather apparently invented the tea bag, so it's just salt in the wound as I love a good cup), and everything just falls into place for him in perfect order. It makes me sick, because I try *so* hard and am met with nothing but resistance, and I swear to God one time I literally saw him turn shit into gold. Well, the gold was actually just covered with some manure, but still on a camera it looked *very* impressive. He is Oxford's golden boy, and I'm the pain in their arse.

"Oxford is informing me that Dr Phillip Hurst has been offered a job in America on their recommendation," I say, looking down at the letter again.

"Why are they writing to you?" Griffin asks.

"They've offered me his position until he comes back."

"Oh, well done, June!" the Professor exclaims. "You've been after that for ages."

I look up at the men, all with eager smiles on their faces.

"They aren't really offering it to me," I argue. "They had to choose between me and Professor Stanley. Stanley is out on sabbatical while he gets his hip replaced, so surely it wasn't a tough decision. And they've made it bloody clear it's going back to Phillip when he comes back!"

"Still," Griffin shrugs. "It's something."

"It's a slap in the face is what it is," I shake my head. "I've tried so hard. I've given them my all, and this is how I'm treated."

The room stays silent, I like to think in sympathy of my plight, but most likely none of the men want to set me off.

"What's in America?" Dr Cooke asks.

"They've found something to do with Butch Cassidy and they want Phillip to run the site," I explain.

"Well, you're better off, if you ask me," the Professor nods knowingly. "No self-respecting, British archaeologist would go to the land of sex, drugs, and rock and roll for their first dig. It's too garish."

"And I've only just moved in," Griffin puts his arm around me and squeezes. "So it wouldn't be a good time for you to go right now anyways."

"And there's no room in our schedule right now," the Professor says. "We've only just got our internship approved. We have to find someone before they change their minds."

He turns to Dr Cooke and nods as they both begin to look over the CVs again, as though my problem is settled.

Settled my foot.

My nostrils flare and I try to contain my anger and keep a level head.

Well, I'm not taking the position, obviously. Let's see what they do when I tell them no and they have no one else. Then we will see who needs whom more.

I storm out of the room and walk over to the phone in the front hall, snatching the receiver off its pedestal and furiously dial the number.

"Professor Dockery's office," the small sing-song voice greets me from the other side of the line.

"Yes, this is Professor June Jenson. I need too speak with Professor Dockery, please."

I hear the gasp from the other side of the phone.

"Professor Jenson, it's me. Julia Graft!" I hear the delighted voice of recognition and quickly place it to the face of one of my bright, yet somewhat flighty, first year students. "Have you had a good summer? Mine's been great so far! My grandfather plays cards with Professor Dockery and got me this intern position, which has been amazing. Though I haven't had a lot of time to spend with my friends, which isn't to say I haven't seen them—"

Remembering Julia had a knack for talking someone's

ear off I quickly cut her off.

"Sounds lovely. Listen, Julia, is Professor Dockery there? I really need to speak with him."

"Oh no, he's gone for the day, I'm afraid," she sounds genuinely regretful. "Is there any message I could leave for him?"

I think back to all the times I heard Julia gossiping with her friends after lecture and think better of leaving the "Sod off!" message I was originally planning.

"Er—no. But please ask him to return my call as soon as he gets in tomorrow."

"Right, will do," she says. "Though it probably won't be until late tomorrow. He has a very important meeting in the morning about Professor Hurst."

"Oh he does, does he?" I say, wrapping my hand more tightly on the receiver.

"Oh yes, have you not heard the exciting news? Professor Hurst is going to be taking a term off and going to America!" Julia explains.

"I'd heard something about that, yes," I mumble.

"Professor Dockery is so excited about it. The Historical Society in the United States has even ordered a television crew to film the whole thing. Professor Hurst is going to be famous!"

Of course he is, the smug bastard.

"A television crew?" I say, as the realization sinks into my stomach. "Is the find expected to be great, then?"

"Oh yes," Julia says, and lowers her voice. "I'm not supposed to say anything, but you *are* from the same department…"

"I won't tell a soul," I say, crossing my fingers behind my back.

"Well, you know that notorious bandit Butch Cassidy? They've made a bunch of films about him—"

"Yes, I know him," I say, trying to move her along.

"Well, they think they've found some sort of lost treasure that he stole. Someone found one of the coins, I believe."

"Who? Where?" I ask, my hands now with a death grip on the receiver.

"I—" she starts and then changes her tone, "Well, hello Professor Millard. Can I help you with something?"

I wait on the line while Julia tells Professor Millard of the Philosophy Department exactly where she suspects Professor Dockery has gone for the afternoon. Judging from the information she is dishing out to everyone today, I'm very glad I didn't give her my earlier message.

I hear her say goodbye and put the receiver back to her lips.

"Professor Jenson?" she asks.

"I'm still here," I reply.

"Oh good. That was just Professor Millard looking for Professor Dockery. She said she wanted to give him some paperwork, though a little birdie recently told me that the two of them are exchanging more then paperwork, if you catch my meaning…"

"Er—wow," I say, unable to think of the right reaction to the news.

"I know, it's shocking if it's true. Can you imagine?"

"Right, well, you were telling me about the coin that was found…" I prompt her.

"Oh, yes. Well that's all I know really," she says regretfully. "I do hope they are able to contact Professor Hurst soon. Professor Dockery is so worried they won't be able to contact him in time."

"Do you know exactly where the coin was found in Colorado?" I ask her.

"It's a private home that the coin was found on. It belongs to a little old lady who owns the property," Julia says.

"Do you have their address? Or a way to contact the Historical Society?" I ask her, before I can chide myself to bite my tongue.

"Er—I'm not sure," she says, and I note the hint of suspicion in her voice and realize I might have gone too far. "Why?"

"Well… er—as a fellow archaeologist, I was just thinking if I come in contact with Professor Hurst before you are able to reach him I could pass along the message," I wait for her reaction.

"You're going to Africa, too?" she asks sceptically.

"I was considering it," I say. "I've heard such great

things from Professor Hurst about this soul trip."

"Retreat," she corrects.

"Yes, retreat, that's right."

"Well, I don't know…" she hedges. "I'm not really supposed to give out that sort of information."

My eyebrows rise, remembering all the other information I have gained from her in the last five minutes.

"Well, I just thought it would help Professor Dockery if I could even do a little preliminary research for Professor Hurst. I mean, he won't have much time when he gets back from Africa before he has to leave. But, no, if you think Professor Dockery has everything under control…"

"Well, there's no harm in a little extra research, is there?" Julia says, and I can almost envision the young girl shrugging away her concerns. "Do you have a pen?"

I quickly scrawl the number as she recites it, and log it into memory.

"So, I'll just give Professor Dockery the message?" she asks.

"Hmm?"

"That you want him to call you back. You had some sort of problem?"

"You know, don't worry about it. I don't want to add to his plate right now. I'll just figure it out myself." I say, and before ringing off I quickly add. "And better not to mention that you gave me this—I think it's just better to surprise him if my research turns up anything. We don't want to get anyone's hopes up."

"Oh yes—right," Julia says. "Probably a good idea. We'll keep it between us girls."

I hang up the phone and look down at the number. A crazy idea circulates in my head. The same thought that prompted me to get the number off of Julia in the first place. I want to stop and think about it, but instead my hand reaches for the phone again.

Ten minutes later I enter the study to find the men in the same positions I left them in, although Griffin is now slumped in the leather chair in the corner and reading CVs.

"This one types at two hundred words per minute. My screenplay could be done in…" he starts mentally counting. "Like three days!"

I walk to the centre of the room and clear my throat.

"So, I have some news," I say, stroking my finger along the edge of the desk.

"Hmm?" the Professor mumbles, not taking his eyes from his paper.

"So, it, er—turns out, I will be going to America," I say it as casually as possible.

"Hmm, good, good," the Professor murmurs and lifts another CV from the pile. "What about this one?"

"Did you hear me?" I ask, taking the paper from him. "I am doing the dig. I am going to America."

"What?" the Professor frowns. "No you're not, they've given it to that Phillip."

"Not anymore," I say, trying to suppress the giggle of excitement that is welling up inside of me. "They've given it to me, instead."

"But, how?" Griffin asks, standing up.

"They, er—changed their minds, I guess," I shrug. "They asked me instead."

"But, why?" the Professor frowns.

"Why not?" I stand up straighter. "Maybe they've finally come to their senses. I have more experience than Phillip. I'm easier to work with."

"Hasn't he done a dozen or so digs already?" Griffin asks, and I choose to ignore his question.

"And all the people at the University speak very highly of him," Dr Cooke adds.

"They've changed their minds!" I repeat. "He's out, and I'm in. I leave in three days."

"Impossible," the Professor says. "I couldn't possibly get away right now."

"Who said I was inviting you?" I turn to Dr Cooke. "You could stay with the Professor for a few weeks, couldn't you?"

"I suppose…" he shrugs, though looks hesitant.

"And Griffin, you could come to America with me," I volunteer. "They're all about films over there, it might bring you some creative inspiration for your screenplay."

And now that I've suggested it, I really warm to the idea. This could just be the chance that we need to get our relationship back on track, away from all our family obligations and hectic schedules.

Griffin thinks about it for a moment, then shakes his head.

"I don't know…" he hedges.

"June dear, I'm not sure you are thinking clearly," the Professor stands up and takes my hand. "You've never been lead on a site before. It is a very large undertaking."

"You had no problem thinking Phillip could do it," I point out, the hurt leaking through my tone.

"And do you really want your first excavation site to be in America? It's so… ostentatious. No, I think the best thing would be for us to find you a lovely little site in England," the Professor smiles at me. "It will be our new intern's first task, right Daniel?"

"Of course," Dr Cooke nods. "Only yesterday I heard of an excavation that's been commissioned in Leeds."

"Who's running that one? Gregory?" the Professor asks.

"Michael Weld, if you can believe it," Dr Cooke shakes his head. "Will be a right cock up from the get go if you ask me."

"There you go!" Griffin stands and wraps his arm around my shoulder. "The Professor will sort you out a dig. You could take the train to Leeds."

I slowly remove his arm from around my shoulder and glare at him.

"I don't need to take the train, because I will be in

America."

"June, be reasonable—" Griffin starts, but I stop him.

"Can I speak to you?" I ask, walking to the doorway. "Alone?"

He looks at the men, raises his eyebrows, and follows me into the hall.

"June, listen, I know you want to go, but I just don't think you are thinking this through. You would be going to *America!* Who would look after the Professor? What about your job?"

"The autumn term doesn't start for another three weeks. If it takes longer I'm sure they would give me a few weeks off," I rub my nose and don't contemplate that it depends on if I still have a job when they find out what I've done. "And Dr Cooke could come and stay here with the Professor. Between him and the home nurse the Professor will be fine while I'm gone."

"And what about us?" Griffin asks, and I can see he is genuinely hurt by my wanting to leave.

"Griffin, I want you to come with me," I say, taking his hand. "This will be our chance to finally have some alone time. We want a future together, but how can we do that when we are always having to look after the Professor and your Mum?"

"I just don't think—" he starts. "We can't just *leave* them. What if we brought them with us?"

"Griffin," I say, shaking my head. "I can't bring them

with me. I will be living at the site. This is my job. It's my *dream*. This is my chance to do something for *me*. How can you ask me not to go?"

Griffin rubs his hand on the back of his neck.

"Please," I plead with him, putting my hands on either side of his face. "Let's do this together."

"I—"

"Griffin?" We hear the call from outside the open front door before Ruth pops her head through the opening. "Oh, there you are. June, love, how's the move coming along?"

I lower my hands and smile in her direction. "Fine. Thanks, Ruth."

"Has—er—everything been unpacked?"

She has a very innocent tone to her voice as she peers over the edge of the boxes.

"Not quite. I didn't know you were stopping by," I say, looking to Griffin, who has an apprehensive look on his face.

"Well, Griffin forgot his wub-wub and he hasn't slept a day without it since he was born," Ruth says, coming towards me in her curlers. She holds up a ratty-old bunny who's missing an eye.

"How… er—*kind*," I say as she hands Griffin the rabbit.

"I'm just glad I was in the neighbourhood and could bring it. It's important for Griffin to feel comfortable in his new home. Did er—" she pauses. "Did the two of you get a chance to talk yet?"

"We have," I say, knowing full well what she is referring

to.

"Wonderful," she says, clapping her hands together.

"Well?" I ask, turning to him. "What's it going to be?"

"Er—" he looks from his Mum to me. He's actually sweating. Unbelievable.

"What's wrong, love?" Ruth asks, looking at Griffin with wide, innocent eyes.

"We were just talking and—" he stops, and at least has the decency to look ashamed of himself.

Well, that's it then. I have my answer. I try and push back the tears in my eyes as my throat begins to burn.

"I'm—I'm going to America," I manage to choke out and force a smile on my face. "I've invited Griffin to go, but—"

"*America?*" Ruth looks shocked and quickly looks to Griffin for reassurance.

"Don't worry, he's not coming," I say to her, continuing to smile as my lips tremble.

"I didn't say—" Griffin reaches for my arm. "What I mean is, it's a big decision…"

Ruth comes to stand closer to Griffin. I look up at him and see the struggle on his face as he tries to find a way to please both of us. Ruth looks at him with tears in her eyes and I realize that I am doing exactly what I just had a go at Ruth for doing all morning. I look from him to Ruth, and I realize that this is it. This is going to be the next fifty years of my life—God knows she'll live that long just to spite me—

unless I do something about it right now.

Taking a deep breath I take a step back.

"It will be fine. It was a lot to ask, and it isn't fair to ask you to drop everything for me. I'll go to America, and you can stay here and work on your screenplay. It'll be fine," I repeat. "*We'll* be fine."

"June, wait—"

I put my hand up to stop him speaking.

"Griffin, it's okay."

I walk up the stairs to my bedroom and gently close the door.

"Does this mean you're coming home?" I can hear Ruth in the front hall.

"Mum, not now!"